# ANGELA

Simon Shelley, his marriage in ruins and his business in trouble, goes to London to meet a rather special kind of call-girl, in an effort to forget his problems for a while. But the meeting with Angela proves to be a major turning point for him, and soon he is on the track of the business people who set out to wreck him. However, the consequent tragic price proves far higher than he expected to pay . . .

STEVE HANNA

# ANGELA

*Complete and Unabridged*

**LINFORD**
*Leicester*

First published in Great Britain in 1983 by
Robert Hale Limited
London

First Linford Edition
published 2003
by arrangement with
Robert Hale Limited
London

British Library CIP Data

Hanna, Steve
  Angela.—Large print ed.—
  Linford mystery library
  1. Detective and mystery stories
  2. Large type books
  I. Title
  823.9'14 [F]

  ISBN 0–7089–9480–6

Published by
F. A. Thorpe (Publishing)
Anstey, Leicestershire

Set by Words & Graphics Ltd.
Anstey, Leicestershire
Printed and bound in Great Britain by
T. J. International Ltd., Padstow, Cornwall

This book is printed on acid-free paper

# 1

Simon Shelley gazed blankly from the carriage window at the passing scene as the train swayed and clattered its way through Clapham Junction.

London! To him it was a totally uninspiring place and, seen from the train as a barren waste of brick and slate, a depressing sight. Only undiluted bloody-mindedness was taking him into the city which he steadfastly refused to refer to as 'Town' and which he insisted he did not journey 'Up' to or 'Down' from. He began to regret being persuaded that he should make the trip, the purpose of which was more a spite against his former wife, Marion, than a conscious effort to satisfy a personal desire or need.

Adultery was not his scene and never had been, yet Marion had obtained the divorce on grounds of adultery when she had known his evening with Rachel Fuhrmann had been business — pure business. Marion had hired a private detective whose armour-plated conscience had permitted him to swear on a small mountain of bibles that Simon had been indulging in extra-marital athletics with Rachel.

Marion could so easily have gone for 'irretrievable breakdown of the marriage' — Simon would have gone along with that because it was so close to reality — but no, she'd persisted in trying to prove a palpable lie was in fact the truth.

Simon or his counsel might well have chosen to risk calling Rachel to give evidence on his behalf, and she might even have been willing, but only a fool would have called her. Her record as what used to be called a 'man-killer' and willing co-respondent would have been a bonus for Marion's counsel. But the situation had been bad enough without laying gifts at his feet.

'To hell with it!' he thought. 'Why bother with recriminations? I'm better off out of that rattle-trap of a marriage!'

Even then he felt no better about the purpose of the London trip. He was rushing headlong into an appointment with a call-girl solely because it proved to be his simplest way to make a gesture at Marion. Even the selection of the girl had been accomplished by proxy — Abe Rousker had laid-on the whole thing for him, and he felt helpless, gauche and confused.

Simon left the train at Victoria, feeling cold and miserable — as much due to his state of mind as from the damp, chill and blustery weather. The bars of the Grosvenor beckoned and a double whisky warmed him; a second set him up for the walk he intended making to limber up his train-atrophied legs.

He set off along Buckingham Palace Road, lighting a panatella as he strolled along, slowly relaxing the tensions of the journey and the aftermath of prolonged marital strife, legal bickerings and uncertainty.

Not for the first time since the storm had burst over him, he muttered into the butt of a cigar: 'I'd dearly love to know just how Marion came to get her story about Rachel and me so pat, so detailed, so believable.'

Conjecture was pointless, nothing was going to reunite them even if he solved the mystery of the skilled perjury and placed his evidence before a judge. What motive had he for trying to reverse the court's decision? He'd had Marion; they were hopelessly incompatible, and restoration of the marriage, while possibly good for his ego, would do nothing now for the family unit.

Family unit? Simon could barely avoid giving an ironic laugh. He and Marion were as oil and water; Sarah loved her father dearly, but she was a fourteen-year-old, growing towards maturity and more in need of a mother's guidance than that of a father.

They were better off divided; at least the incessant warfare was only a remembered bitter ordeal and the nights in bed beside Marion, who might as well have not been there, no longer a torment. At least Sarah could go home from school and find a quiet place, and live a life untroubled by the angry exchanges between her parents.

Having eaten at a restaurant along the Strand and failed to satisfy his palate or his stomach, he walked on towards his appointment.

At last he came to the great towering block of concrete, stone and glass which seemed more suitable for offices than apartments; it reared up out of a paved court, stark against the sky whose moving clouds gave him the impression that the massive grey edifice was about to fall upon him. He looked at the doorway, took his courage in both hands and went inside to find himself in an outer foyer, the doors before him and behind were of armoured glass, tough as steel, more transparent than gossamer. The inner set securely locked so that he could not go farther.

To his right, Simon saw the notice board listing floor numbers, flat numbers and the names of residents. He searched for the one he wanted and pressed the button labelled 'Angela Whitney'.

'Yes? Who is it?' asked a canned and somewhat breathless voice.

'Simon Shelley,' he said. 'Abe Rousker —'

'Hello, Mr Shelley,' the voice cut in brightly. 'Come on up.'

The electric lock on the inner doors clicked sharply. Simon pushed and, feeling cheap and foolish, walked through into the inner foyer. He felt a panicky wish to cut and run, but could he do so without another word? Not really, it would be unfair to the girl; she was expecting him and for all practical purposes he had arrived. If he now failed to reach her door she would begin to wonder what had become of him. His mind reached forward in time to examine all the embarrassing possibilities consequent upon running away, and he found he was unable to face them.

Simon fingered the button to call the lift, stepped inside when it came and selected the seventh floor. His belly seemed to sink momentarily with the 'G' force and then he was swept upwards.

At the seventh floor he stepped from the lift to find himself at one end of a long, broad corridor stretching away across the breadth of the building. Simon set off in search of 715. Each move he made in the building was performed with a nervous reluctance, but he pressed forward despite his inhibitions — and then he found the number and stood before the door, uncertain and afraid.

Behind him, somewhere, a door-latch clicked. Startled, he turned and saw a man duck hurriedly back into the flat from which he had appeared. Simon's nervousness vented itself in an odd chuckle. Taken in a sudden mood of mischief, he continued on up the corridor, found a service staircase and stood back in it, waiting. He told himself it was a stupid impulse and a rotten trick to play upon a man probably as ashamed as he was.

Again a door-latch clicked. Simon peeped cautiously and saw a cascade of chestnut hair at the door where the man's face had appeared. Low voices reached him, the words indiscernible, then the man reappeared, flung hurried glances to left and right and scurried briskly towards the lift.

The man was smartly dressed. A good-quality topcoat was cut on the lines of a British Warm and the trousers showing beneath it gave adequate indication of an expensive, well-cut suit. Simon thought he should know the man, but the elegant attire seemed inappropriate to the half-remembered image, and he rejected the notion.

★　★　★

Angela Whitney opened her door within seconds of Simon pressing the bellpush. A natural blonde with deep blue eyes, her hair was drawn back into a pony-tail. She wore a navy wing-collared jacket and navy print shirt-blouse with an off-white skirt. Simon thought her beautiful — breathtaking, in fact. He was barely aware that he had been envisaging a painted face and a blousy figure; all he knew was that never in his wildest dreams would this girl have stood before him as she then did in reality.

'Miss Whitney?' he asked doubtingly.

She gave a warm, disarming smile. It was a pleasant, natural exercise of facial muscles and eyes which were frank, open and humorous. Simon thought her quite delightful.

'Please come in, Mr Shelley,' she invited, her voice pitched low naturally. 'Did you lose your way? It's taken you quite a while to reach here.'

Simon entered the little hallway, and the girl closed the door before leading him through to a comfortably furnished lounge. She walked gracefully with an easy swing of her legs, and Simon began to forget some, at least, of his misgivings.

'I very nearly chickened-out, for starters,' he admitted shamefaced. 'And then a chap who was about to come out of a doorway across the corridor seemed embarrassed to see someone standing there and ducked back inside. I went along to the service stairs and kept out of sight to enable him to get away incognito.'

'From Mira's?' Angela asked, smiling. '718 — to the left of my door as you go out?'

He thought about it. 'Is this Mira a girl with long chestnut hair?' Simon asked.

'Yes, that's her. Her friend is a mite bashful. Quite a nice chap, though I

9

wouldn't be surprised if he could be a bit starchy in different company.'

'I had the feeling I should know the man,' Simon led.

She shook her head. 'Sorry. You can tell me whatever you wish while you're here, but once you've left no one will ever learn from me anything you've spoken about, nor your name or address. Abe should've warned you.'

'He did. It's just that I forgot for the moment.' Simon felt the tension creeping back into his system.

Angela looked at him, quizzically appraising. 'Would you like a drink — or a cup of coffee? I missed lunch today through shopping and I barely got back in time to let you in. The coffee-pot is on.'

'Coffee, if I may,' Simon decided, adding: 'If you have something for your lunch, don't worry about me, you eat.'

She chuckled deep in her throat. 'And wouldn't you look down your nose if I did,' she said, making for the kitchen and calling over her shoulder: 'Cigarettes on the coffee-table!'

Simon opened the gold cigarette box,

took out a king-size, filter-tipped cigarette. 'One for you?' he called.

'Yes, please.'

He picked up a second cigarette, carried it to the kitchen door, passed it to the girl and lit both.

'I really shouldn't smoke in the kitchen,' she admitted conspiratorially, 'but, as it's only coffee — '

'Please,' Simon urged, 'I honestly wouldn't mind if you had a meal.'

'I often miss lunch,' Angela replied with a firm shake of her head. 'I make a virtue of it and call those days my fast-days.'

When the coffee was ready they sat at opposite ends of the settee to drink their coffee, the girl, her sleek legs elegantly crossed, tried to set him at ease.

'How is Abe?' she asked. 'The last time he was here we went out to dinner and he ate something which didn't agree with him.'

Simon grinned. 'He's as fit as a flea. He must be, because he's moaning about how poor business is, how ill he is, etc., etc. I've heard nothing of a lawsuit, though.'

The girl frowned, perplexed, anxious in case her guest was leading her on to reveal something. 'Lawsuit?' she asked cautiously.

'Yes. Can you see Abe allowing someone to feed him bad food without him then trying to sue them for everything down to the fillings in their teeth?'

Angela's face erupted into bright sunshine as she laughed outright. 'Poor Abe,' she said. 'How frustrating to be unable to prove anything.'

It was Simon's turn to be puzzled. 'Frustrating?'

She swallowed another chuckle. 'He'd spent a couple of days here with me, relaxing and unburdening himself. Can you imagine him in a courtroom with Becky at his side while I took the stand to give evidence on his behalf? Becky may turn a blind eye in private, but how would she react if our arrangement became public knowledge?'

Simon watched her closely as he observed pointedly: 'I understood you to say you didn't talk about your clients.'

Angela's smile never slipped. 'Abe says he knows you, likes you and trusts you. The odd thing about him is that when he says that of someone it's a certainty that the other person feels the same about him. A good man is our Abe, a good man. So it's equally certain you know Becky Rousker and, knowing her, you'll be able to understand.'

Simon nodded. 'It figures,' he acknowledged.

'There's nothing terribly wrong in this set-up,' Angela defended. 'I fill a need Becky can no longer meet. Admittedly there's a business element in our relationship but there's also a lot of real affection.'

She finished her coffee, saw that Simon had also finished, and rose to her feet. 'Come along,' she directed briskly, 'I'll wash-up, you dry.'

* * *

Simon emerged very slowly from a deep and relaxing sleep, he turned his head into the pillow and realized his cheek pressed against a firm breast. He opened his eyes and saw Angela's lovely eyes looking down at him cradled in her arms. She appeared happy, like a proud mother with a recently fed and contented infant.

He drew down her head towards his and kissed her long and tenderly. 'You're the most beautiful and most efficient psychiatrist I know,' he whispered.

'Applied theory,' she explained softly. 'Talk may be all very well, but if Freud had the right of it, the best treatment is a little love judiciously applied.'

'I love your theory, too,' he murmured, moving to take her in his own arms.

'Love?' Angela asked, frowning through her smile.

'A touchy point?' Simon guessed.

Angela shook her head. 'Not exactly,' she replied. 'It's just that I wouldn't want you to imagine yourself to be in love with me. This patient-nurse, patient-doctor fixation is a common hazard. Merely because someone pulls off some sort of 'rescue act', the rescued person shouldn't become unduly attached on that account.

I don't believe a saved life then belongs to the rescuer.'

He kissed her again, surprised that he had found it so easy to forget that in law she was 'a common prostitute'. Then again, there was nothing common about Angela, and the form of prostitution practised by her appeared to be vastly different from that conjured up by the description. He sought words with which to explain to himself how he saw her and her occupation.

Angela seemed to pick up his thoughts for she murmured softly: 'I have a great capacity for giving affection. I need people to lavish it on. I'm a long way from being a nymphomaniac and I couldn't make physical love with anyone for whom I didn't care. You know how it is with people who care for children — their love fairly exudes from their pores. I suppose I'm a little like that except that I care for men — men for whom modern life is a strain, a burden, weighing them down with worry and stress. I provide a peaceful oasis in a storm-ridden desert.'

'D'you know,' Simon admitted, 'I'm not going to like leaving you — not one little bit.'

'Please, Simon,' Angela begged, 'try not to become too attached. In any case, you don't have to go, surely? Not yet?'

'You'll want me out of here soon,' Simon suggested.

'I understood that you'd be able to stay until tomorrow,' said Angela, and Simon thought he could detect a note of disappointment in her tone, but he dismissed the idea at once as being the work of his ego.

'Well, of course I'd love to stay,' he said, 'if I may.'

'I want you to.' She sounded nervous.

Simon wondered if it really had been his ego which had made him suspect the disappointment. 'Until when?' he asked.

Angela made a frown of mock concentration. 'Take me to lunch tomorrow,' she replied, 'and then I'll see you off on your train.'

'Is that usual?' he asked.

'Is what usual?'

'You, seeing fellows off.'

'I'll answer that question tomorrow,' she promised and snuggled up against him.

'Well, if we have plenty of time,' said Simon, 'what about doing something this evening?'

'Such as?'

'Dinner?' he suggested. 'A show?'

'We *could* eat here,' Angela offered. 'I'm a pretty fair cook.'

Simon shook his head. 'That wouldn't be fair. I'm partly the cause of you missing your lunch so it's only right and proper I should take you out somewhere.'

Angela smiled up at him. 'All right,' she agreed, 'we'll go out. But I'll pick the place. It's good and inexpensive. But we'll skip the show.'

He looked down into her eyes, reading the message there. 'Yes,' he affirmed, 'we'll skip the show.'

Her lips parted slightly and reached up for his.

They kissed tenderly, and Angela's heart fluttered in panic as she began to realize what was happening to her. The pressure of their lips increased and

Simon's gentle hands began caressing her body, exploring her neck and shoulders before moulding her firm young breasts in his palms.

'You're beautiful,' he whispered.

'I want to please you,' Angela murmured.

'You please me. My God, *how* you please me.'

Words ceased to have meaning, their bodies met, blended and became one as they made love once more.

\* \* \*

The train surged under a burst of power from the electric motors, heaved off to the left and slowed sharply. Henry Rhodes winced as his head bucked against the edge of the window frame whose corner was sharp enough to convince him he'd broken the skin of his scalp.

He put his hand to his head, gently fingering the tender flesh but finding no trace of blood. Only the barest trace of hair-cream showed on his fingers and the faint perfume of it sent his mind flying off

18

to recollections of the previous evening and especially to Mira Feaney. For a fleeting moment a smile broke across his grim face and flickered on his lips only to slip away again unnoticed by his travelling companions as his thoughts moved on to the unexpected encounter with the not-so-strange stranger in the corridor outside Mira's flat.

The memory of that moment triggered a train of conjecture about why the chance meeting had stirred in him so much panic. And he had panicked — uncharacteristically but definitely — there was no denying the truth. Never before had he seen the man in that place and yet his immediate reaction had been that of a rabbit sensing the presence of danger. But why? Was the man really unknown to him or was he merely overreacting because of the amusing tale Mira had spun in her soft Irish voice? A tale of a man caught out by a detective hired by his wife.

No. That was not possible. Clair would do nothing like that. Or did he just hope Clair would do no such thing. What if the man had been a detective checking up on him? It was an ever-present risk with which he had been forced to live, but if he were to be discovered it would be better by far that the finger should point at Mira Feaney than Marion Shelley. Until her decree could be made absolute it was essential that Marion should be protected. Later, if he should feel the need to free himself of Clair's claustrophobic grip on his life, he could arrange to be discovered but, in the meantime, he was confident he could leave the termination of his marriage to nature's tender care.

His wife — chubby, apparently unassuming and long-suffering, but beneath that possessive and suffocating — was almost as likely to die as the train rattled across the next set of points as she was to be alive in several years' time. Her heart condition would remove her from the scene in due course; it was a serious condition and only her unruffled attitude had allowed her to cling, however tenuously, to life.

Henry believed that he had loved her well enough until late years when her possessiveness had worn too thin, and he had begun to look elsewhere even before the heart condition showed up. She had borne him a daughter and had been intensely loyal, and for that he continued to feel responsible for her even though his greatest desire was to be rid of her. He did not wish her dead, but faced the imminent probability of it with a business-like phlegm rather than equanimity. A little morosely, perhaps, he returned to working on the mystery of the man in the corridor outside Mira Feaney's flat.

Who was the fellow? And did he really recognize him from some unspecified time or place? Had the man's business in the corridor been genuine or was he just a prying eye? Had he been followed from Beverington? Most importantly, had the man really been interested in *him?*

The two-hour train journey terminated at Beverington Central with Henry still not clear in his mind about the stranger. Absently he hefted his two big suitcases and set out to walk around by backstreets to his office.

# 2

Angela Whitney turned slowly in the bed, stretching luxuriously, and then, smiling contentedly, snuggled against the man beside her. She was more than a little surprised at herself and the way she felt about Simon Shelley. Her whole way of life had been geared to providing relaxation for a small number of provincial businessmen, easing strained nerves and providing satisfaction for their deprived natural instincts, and she had taken genuine pleasure from her ability to succeed. As often as not they had needed mothering as much as the sexual satisfaction; few gave anything of themselves despite the fact that for the most part they were kind and generous men. If they had not been kind and considerate she could never have gone through with it no matter what the financial rewards.

She took great delight in her ability to give so wholly of herself for the benefit of others, but it was itself a burden soothing away the work or emotional cares of others, relieved only from time to time when no-one called. With Simon, though, she was conscious of something very different about it all, something special — delightful, refreshing, yet vaguely worrying.

Angela cast her mind back to his arrival on the previous afternoon. Simon had begun nervously and she had reacted in much the same manner as she had with others similarly uncomfortable in her presence. But then there had been that first act of love-making and he had set out to please her rather than simply making demands on her. He had then relaxed in her company, and their relationship had become closer to that of lovers. Simon had assumed a protective rôle as would any young man for his girl. It was an experience almost unknown to her, and she felt secure as his strong encircling arm drew her close until their naked bodies met at every possible point.

She kissed him tenderly, accepting the stubble on his face as the norm for any morning but, this time, allowing her lips to linger on the bristles. All too often in the past Angela would have felt physically and emotionally drained at such a moment, but on that day she was totally at ease, fresh, bright, alert and recharged. She knew that for the first time she had received in kind as much as — or more than — she gave, and it was an enriching experience.

With considerable reluctance Angela studied the bedside clock.

'Nine-thirty,' she murmured. 'Breakfast?'

'I could murder it,' Simon admitted, 'but there are other hungers.'

Angela smiled happily and kissed him again. 'Eat first, play later,' she parodied.

'Will there be time?' he asked earnestly.

'We'll make time,' she said huskily, 'I promise.'

Regretfully, Simon permitted her to move from his embrace and watched her sweet, firm young body disappear into a blue housecoat before she left the bedroom.

Whatever name should properly be

used to describe Angela's profession, Simon knew that for as long as he lived he would never be able to think of her that way. He had arrived nervously, burdened with a sense of guilt, soon he would have to leave, but his departure would be marked with intense regret and that regret would not stem from the ending of their sexual relationship — deeply satisfying though that had been — but from the emotional rapport between them and especially the girl's tremendous ability to give so much of her inner self.

He lay back against the pillows reliving the delights of the past few hours — the candlelight dinner, the tender love-making, the companionship. And then, out of the blue, came the image of the stranger playing 'jack-in-the-box' at the door of the flat opposite. He was sure he should know that man. Still ruminating on the incident, Simon rose from the bed and took his turn in the bathroom before dressing as far as his shirt and trousers and going through to the lounge.

'D'you work with Abe?' Angela asked,

emerging from the kitchen, unconscious of the gapping housecoat revealing a length of sleek leg.

Simon shook his head, clearing it and answering the question. His stomach flipped, but he failed to relate the reaction to the sight of the girl or to the smell of cooking with any certainty. 'No,' he managed to reply. 'Abe's in wholesale, I'm in information.'

'Information?' she asked cautiously. 'What sort of information?'

'Business investigations, research — that sort of thing.'

Angela's tiny frown reappeared and her eyes showed her concern as she asked: 'Are you a private detective?'

He smiled reassuringly. 'Not the sort you have in mind,' he said, 'and I'm certainly not here on business, in any case.'

'I don't like private detectives as a race,' she declared flatly, disillusion showing in her expression.

'I'm not overfond of them myself,' he returned ruefully as his smile slipped away. He shrugged resignedly and once more felt the burdens of the world settle upon his shoulders. 'I'd better go,' he said with an infinite sadness and began to move towards the bedroom door, intent upon gathering up his meagre belongings.

Alarm leapt onto Angela's lovely face and tears filled her blue eyes. She moved quickly into his path, turned, took his hands and gazed into his eyes. 'No,' she begged huskily, 'you mustn't go — not like this. I hurt you then and I wouldn't have had that happen for the world. Simon, sweet tender Simon, you're so like a small frightened boy in many ways, terribly vulnerable and almost too afraid to seize happiness for fear it's not yours to have and someone will snatch it back at any moment. Is that the real reason you were sent to me? Has happiness been snatched from your grasp before?'

Simon placed his arms around her and clung to her tightly. 'You could say that,' he agreed, 'though often it seems I've never really known what it was.'

'Happiness?'

'Happiness,' Simon affirmed, and then, noting again the smell of grilling bacon, he asked: 'Shouldn't you see to that?'

Angela turned away with some annoyance that the bacon's demands were more immediate than Simon's needs. She felt a sudden clutch of fear that the breaking of contact might give him the time to draw his protective shell more closely about him. Brushing the tears from her eyes and cheeks, she dealt briskly with the grill, the toast and coffee, then carried them through to the dining-space.

Simon followed her to the table, sat down at his place and began picking at the food.

'Don't lose your appetite,' Angela begged anxiously. 'I've said the wrong thing, I know, and it's upset you, but you should eat.'

Simon nodded but continued to mount only a half-hearted assault upon the breakfast he had so urgently desired such a short while before. 'You were asking about happiness,' he said musingly. 'I believe that in married life I've never enjoyed it. Marion and I married in haste and much too early — for which act Marion lays all blame upon me. I make no pretence to be blameless, so, of course, I accept a fair share of the responsibility. Marion would have me shoulder it all!'

'Marion? She's your wife?'

'Yes. Or, to be precise, she *was*.'

'You're divorced? I didn't know — Abe said nothing. D'you miss her?'

Simon's smile was ironic, and a fragile thing instantly fragmented by a brief shake of his head. 'Not in the way you may think,' he replied. 'It has come more as a sense of relief.'

'You divorced her?'

'No. The reverse.'

'You gave her grounds?'

'Not in reality. I left myself vulnerable by accident.'

'You should talk about it,' Angela urged, 'you *need* to.'

'After our daughter Sarah was born,' Simon explained, 'the 'shutters went up' as they say. I thought I understood. Adjustment; temporary preoccupation with the baby; a little trouble at the birth — '

'Much trouble?' Angela cut in solicitously.

'None at all! But I discovered that much later — five years later or thereabouts. Marion's continuing frigidity worried me so I spoke to our doctor, explaining just as I've explained to you. He assured me the birth had been smooth and easy. Even so, I accept that the mother's rôle is painful, uncomfortable and wearing. I looked around for a valid reason for her attitude and all I could think of was that Marion resented the loss of freedom; the filling out of her figure; and the assumed loss of desirability.'

'She never adjusted? Never made love again?'

Simon shrugged helplessly. 'Nothing.'

'I find marriage a trifle frightening,' Angela confessed. 'I'm afraid that I, too, might become frigid — perhaps as a reaction against this life. If I were to marry, I would want to continue loving my man and be loved by him, and the thought that producing a child could possibly be the factor which divides rather than unites us horrifies me. Perhaps that's why I am as I am. This way I can give love without fear of letting down a partner tied to me for life.'

'It happens,' Simon acknowledged sadly, 'as I know well enough, but I doubt if such a thing could happen to you. You have that vast and wonderful capacity to love and, with the spur of that underlying fear, you would see to it that your love was evenly distributed between husband and child, or children.'

'Yet your experience shows — ' Angela began.

'That Marion was young,' Simon interposed quickly, 'resentful and selfish; that I was young, inexperienced and resentful!'

For some time Angela ate in silence, her thoughts ranging back and forth over what Simon had told her. 'How did your wife come to obtain evidence against you?' she asked at last. 'You said that in reality you gave her no grounds.'

'It began as a matter of business,' he explained. 'A client needed some business information and a useful contact was a young woman named Rachel Fuhrmann. The only appointment I could arrange with her was a late evening one. The snag was that she has a reputation for being an easy lay — an eager lay. I was observed coming and going, times were recorded and I was hoist.'

'Hoist?'

'Hoist with my own petard — blown up by my own gun, if you like. I, an investigator was caught, if 'caught' is the correct word, by another of my kind.'

'If what you did was in all inno-cence — ' Angela began.

'You're suggesting that I could success-fully have contested the suit? On the face of it, I could, but then Rachel Fuhrmann would not have been inclined to attend court on my behalf. In the first place she was no friend of mine, and in any case she would have been manna from heaven to Marion's counsel who was as good as they come. I felt only that I owed it to myself to make a show of defence and to record my side of it in court, beyond that I found I couldn't care less. I wasn't the guilty party. I wasn't walking out on Marion and Sarah, I was being got rid of and, so far as I could judge, I'd be a sight better off out of it.'

'But it still hurts.'

'Some of it,' he admitted. 'The railroading; the partial loss of Sarah; the sense of abdicating my responsibility.'

'*Did* you abdicate any responsibility?'

'Not that I know of — not consciously,' Simon replied uncertainly. 'But I feel that I must have contributed in some way to the breakdown.'

Angela finished her breakfast and sipped at a second cup of coffee. She was angry with herself for hurting Simon with her outburst against private investigators. She knew that outburst to have had its origins in her dread of letting down one of her regulars by allowing him to be caught in a compromising situation. She should have known that Abe Rousker was too wily a bird to send a cuckoo into her nest. Simon was as much in need of her comfort as any of those others for whom she was maintained in her flat. More — she felt a disturbing need for him. Unaccustomed to such an experience, she interpreted it in a sexual context.

'I'm sorry I was so hasty,' she offered helplessly.

'Honest,' he corrected, and his smile was there once more.

'You really *are* different,' Angela declared. 'You're not the kind of man I fear, you're — ' She set down her cup, took his hand and led him from the table.

★   ★   ★

'I'm off to the wholesalers,' Rhodes barked, glaring fiercely at young Todd. 'Try to get the place tidied up and treat the customers with civility. You are not here to do them a favour but to sell them a good article at a fair price — they do *us* the favours when they bring their custom to us.'

'I can't fawn!' the young man growled surlily.

'No one expects you to, but, if you consider my methods fawning, I suggest you look elsewhere for employment!'

The shaft went home, the recession had stretched the dole queues too far for comfort.

Rhodes added no more, he felt it would be gilding the lily. He walked to the shop door, opened it, turned and favoured his new assistant with a fierce glare, his eyes speaking volumes. He left the shop and hurried off among the passing shoppers.

Todd watched him out of sight then gestured childishly with two upraised fingers. With Rhodes unable to see the signal of derision he felt safe enough and turned aggressively towards the back of the shop. Promptly he slammed his left shin against a prominently displayed coffee-table; he swore luridly and fluently.

Henry Rhodes continued along his way at a brisk walk, rounding the corner at the end of the street and crossing the side-street diagonally to an alley which he entered and passed along to a doorway set in a broad, high blank wall. The door had been meagrely coated with a black paint which had found the damp oak unattractive and was trying, desperately, to peel away. It was the only entrance to Beaver (Wholesale) Limited. He let himself in and climbed up a worn wooden staircase to a small suite of down-at-heel offices.

He tapped on the outer door as he entered; it was a gesture, no more.

'Good morning, Mr Rhodes,' said the girl behind the only desk set back from the small counter. She was short, squat, unprepossessing, efficient. 'It's a nice day.'

'Yes,' Rhodes agreed shortly. He stabbed a finger at the inner door. 'Is Mrs Shelley in?'

'Yes, sir, but she's on the telephone just now. If you'll have a seat.'

With ill grace Henry sat on the hard chair on the 'wrong' side of the counter and contained himself in thinning patience until Marion should be free. He could afford to allow the girl to see him thus, she would see it as typical of him and well suited to his image of irritability. The important thing was that she should not know that he was 'the company chairman' whose instructions were passed on by Mrs Shelley, and neither should she be given the opportunity of discovering his relationship with Marion.

At last the telephone gave a final 'ting'

as Marion rang off. The girl rose and tapped on the inner door, waited to be bidden and then opened the door to announce: 'Mr Rhodes is here.'

'Oh! Ask him to come in, please, Jean,' he heard Marion say, the sound of her voice sending a tingle up his spine. He rose from his chair, lifted the counter-flap and entered the office as the girl stood aside.

'Good morning, Mrs Shelley,' Rhodes opened brusquely.

'And good morning to you, Mr Rhodes,' Marion replied brightly as the girl closed the door.

Rhodes glanced over his shoulder as though to be sure the girl had not remained in the room and then he looked back at Marion, a warm smile taking command of his features, softening and humanizing them.

'My dear — ' Rhodes opened his arms wide and she came into them, throwing her own arms about his neck. He held her tightly and they kissed hungrily. 'I've missed you,' he breathed in her ear, at the same time making mental reservations because of his pleasurable night with Mira Feaney.

'No more than I've missed you,' Marion replied softly, resting secure in his arms. She saw him as a warm, loving and undemanding man, quite the opposite of what she had inferred from his business image before she got to know him personally. It was this marked contrast in him which, having discovered by accident, she found so attractive. But it was equally fortunate that she was not aware that he had known of her as an icy-hearted woman whose sole aim in life was self-gratification.

A single smile from him, an open gesture from her, had begun their friendship — a friendship which had warmed, broadened and deepened.

'I've brought you something,' he said, indicating his briefcase.

'You shouldn't have.'

'Nevertheless,' he smiled, 'it's here and it's for you. But, if you don't like it — '

Marion was moved by the tenderness of him, by his concern lest his gift prove displeasing and his calm acceptance that it might. So different from Simon who had brought little gifts from time to time only to be angry when she rejected them. It had never occurred to her that perhaps his anger was directed more at the manner of her refusal than at the refusal itself.

Henry Rhodes had never met Simon, of that Marion was pretty certain, and, indeed, he was insistent that he had no wish to meet him. She and Simon had been so much younger, of course, when they met — he, in her view at least, more so than herself in terms of maturity. He had been handsome, impetuous and persuasive, and Marion had been over-whelmed and flattered by his gaiety and vitality, but never had she succumbed to his persuasiveness; she had chosen both time and place, and for her own reasons.

No, try though she might, latterly, there had been no way in which she could justify her current claim that Simon had seduced her, virtually against her will, before their marriage. It had been her jealous possessiveness which had led them into marriage — a wedding of convenience of a sort, but of her own making. In their group of friends Simon had been the real 'catch', and at one time it had seemed that Sylvia Donald was fishing to greatest effect.

Sylvia was not averse to fishing with her body as bait, and Simon was a virile young man — he ceased all attempts to seduce Marion.

She had felt him slipping away and believed that Sylvia was winning. In the end it was Marion who seduced Simon and she won on a pregnancy, not love, but at least Sylvia Donald had been beaten.

Marion believed that Henry Rhodes cared about her, not merely her body. He had an ailing wife, a daughter apparently bent upon making a career of being a spinster, and he seemed to need her, Marion, in a way Simon had never done.

Suddenly aware that she had been daydreaming and that Henry had gone unanswered, 'I'm sure I shall like it,' she assured him happily. 'Show me, please, and I'll set your mind at rest.'

Henry smiled down into her eyes and then, with a conjurer's flourish, produced from his briefcase a small blue leather-bound box.

Marion's heart leapt as she pressed the catch.

Diamonds glinted brilliantly at her from the ring's cushioned resting-place, their sharp little facets winking and flashing enthusiastically even in the poor light of the drab office, seeming to bring the place to life.

'Henry,' she gasped at this manifestation of his hidden generosity. 'Oh, Henry.'

His eyes had not wavered from her face. The ring had cost a tidy sum, but to his mind it's true value could be gauged only by its effect upon Marion, and he felt the relief well up inside him as he observed her almost girlish wonder and delight.

★   ★   ★

Angela clung tightly to Simon. Never had she so dreaded the moment of parting from a man. She knew, agonizingly, that a girl with her way of life — honestly, cleanly and loyally though she conducted it — would never be able to hold a man like Simon Shelley.

He would have been able to hold her — withdraw her to a more conventional existence and enable her to turn her back upon her current lifestyle without the least regret. But she knew with a cold disheartening certainty that he would never try.

Because of her commitment to other men, she found her emotions confused and uncertain. She wanted Simon physically and emotionally with a great longing, and he was the first man ever to affect her in that way. Her way of life had given her a yardstick by which to measure love against lust, yet it served only to make her unsure and distrustful of her own feelings.

'What will you do when you get back to Beverington?' Angela asked, as much to divert her thoughts as to seek any real information.

Simon smiled ruefully. 'Get down to some work,' he replied. '*If* anyone'll employ me now.'

'And why wouldn't they?' she posed,

prepared to spring to his defence.

'An investigator beaten at his own game?' he scoffed. 'The headlines were bad enough without the verbal ridicule. I'm not 'up tight' about that; on the face of it it was fair comment, but it's done me no good businesswise.'

'But you were making no efforts to conceal your actions when — ' Angela's voice trailed off as she experienced great difficulty in considering or discussing his divorce — it made her think of his ex-wife and she felt strong and confused emotions in that regard.

'True,' Simon acknowledged her point, 'but who's to convince my customers — standing or potential?'

'Perhaps,' said Angela unaware of a flash of inspiration, 'you could investigate that other investigator.'

# 3

Becky Rousker's face broke into its most open and welcoming smile. 'Simon!' she cried delightedly. 'Come in, come in. How did the break go?'

Simon kissed her cheek as he stepped into the house. 'Fine, Becky, fine,' he assured her.

'You feel better for it?' she pressed.

He had to be careful here. One wrong word and Abe was in trouble. 'Immensely,' he assured her truthfully, adding: 'I feel a different feller altogether.' He grinned broadly in support of his words.

'I should hope you're not!' Becky snorted, leading the way into the lounge. 'I liked the original well enough — always supposing you could rid yourself of all that worry and tension which was turning you into an old grouch!'

'Oh yes,' he assured her, 'the break has achieved that, at least.'

'And how was Angela?' Becky had her back towards him as she spoke. She was pouring two glasses of sherry, and the offhand delivery of the question had the same effect upon him as if she'd kicked him in the genitals.

'An — An — Angela?' He was caught completely off guard, apparently faced with a conflict not of his making and on ground not of his choosing.

'Yes,' said Becky calmly, ignoring his obvious discomfiture. She turned and handed him one of the sherry glasses. 'Angela Whitney. You stayed with her, of course?'

Simon felt that he was wallowing in storm-tossed seas, desperately searching for some straw to cling to and finding nothing.

'Yes,' was the best he could muster, and that lamely and shamefaced.

'Then how was she?' Becky persisted.

Simon gulped at the wine ill-manneredly. 'Nice,' he said, raising his glass to indicate that he referred to the sherry and not the girl.

'Simon, you're evading the question,'

Becky accused. 'How was Angela?'

'Fit,' he replied shortly, still seeking a way out of the trap but finding only a change of subject. 'Is Abe about?'

'Abe's not home,' she said bluntly, 'and won't be for another half-hour yet, so you've plenty of time to tell me about Angela.' There was a twinkle in Becky's dark eyes and a barely suppressed smile played about her full lips.

'I — well — '

'You *did* spend the night with her?' Becky pressed.

Simon nodded dejectedly, a naughty boy caught out.

'Whatever is the matter?' teased Becky. 'You're not embarrassed, surely?'

'Too right I am,' he admitted fiercely, fishing in a pocket for one of his panatella cigars.

She provided him with a light from the handmade brass table lighter bearing a military badge. 'You're afraid of dropping Abe into the soup?' she suggested. 'Don't give it a thought. D'you really imagine I don't know about his little jaunts to London?'

'Well — ' Simon shrugged helplessly — 'I like Abe and I like you — you've both been very good to me. I've just been through the experience of a divorce and it's bloody harrowing, I can tell you. I don't want anything like that for you and Abe so I can't and won't give you any evidence — unless you just want evidence that I was with Angela.'

'So who brought up the subject of divorce?'

'You seemed to be working around to getting me to put the finger on Abe, weren't you?' Simon accused sadly.

'I'll have you know that I was not!' Becky defended indignantly.

'Then what *are* you leading up to?' Simon demanded.

'I'm letting you see that I know and understand about Abe, about you and about Angela.'

Slowly and carefully Simon sat down in an easy-chair. 'You,' he said with the same deliberation, 'are telling me you accept that your husband, Abe, has a liaison with a girl named Angela and that I, too, know her and have been with her? Just what kind of woman are you? Don't you care at all? And I thought you loved Abe!'

'Love? Of course I love him!'

'And yet you show no jealousy, anger or disappointment. I repeat: What kind of woman are you?'

Becky — stocky, her face almost rugged, dark hair greying and wise eyes studying him intently — was a very special kind of woman, and Simon was about to discover just a little of her extra-ordinariness. She sat in another chair and began to explain.

'Abe and I were the victims of an arranged marriage. Our parents were so rigidly orthodox that it hurt, and we were raised to obey. His family and mine were old friends from back at the beginning to time; we visited one another regularly and, as children, Abe and I often played together. We both knew, very early in our lives, that we would eventually be expected to marry each other. We accepted that, lived with it and never considered objecting to it — until it was too late, of course, and we were man and wife.'

'It must have been a good arrangement,' Simon observed, 'it's worked well for all these years.'

'My life! It didn't work on its own, we had to *make* it work! We had no children, though we both love them; I miscarried our first and a whole army of doctors finally decided I should try to have no more. Hopes of a family were dead.'

'You could have adopted.'

'The war broke out soon after we were married, and in 1941 Abe went off with the Yeomanry. We had discussed adoption before he was called up but at that time the yearning for our own was too powerful. Only the marriage vows and family loyalties held Abe and I together at that time, there was no love — and no love-making. When he got leave we found difficulty, physically and emotionally, in making it a real union of two people. Quarrels broke out so frequently on every leave that I began to believe marriage was like the stand-up comic's joke-book. By the time the war was over Abe and I had nothing in common.'

Simon, though deeply saddened by this

outpouring, was nevertheless greatly puzzled by it. 'Yet you stuck together,' he pointed out.

'Yes,' Becky smiled broadly, 'we stuck. It was terribly hard going but eventually we found the magic formula to mutual respect. On my side that respect turned out to be an understanding and acceptance of Abe's physical needs. He was always a virile man and, since I couldn't give him any sexual satisfaction, he sought it elsewhere. Of course, I found out about it and ran through the whole gamut of emotions — hurt pride, anger, tears, despair — but fortunately I had the good sense not to accuse him directly. What he was doing wasn't unnatural. After all, it was really my job to please him. I told myself that over and over again, and knowing that I could no longer bring myself to play my part I faced facts and condoned his little affairs. It worked a miracle!'

'What sort of miracle?' Simon pressed.

'Abe became more affectionate towards me, more understanding, more loyal, more trusting. It was worth the sacrifice of a small quantity of feminine marital pride.'

'And now you're making the point that Marion would have done well to adopt a similar attitude?' Simon suggested.

Becky shook her head and said, 'No. I'm letting you know that I understand Abe and consequently that I also understand you. I dropped enough hints to coax Abe into fixing you up with Angela *and* I explained the whole thing to Angela beforehand.'

'Let me get this straight,' Simon growled disbelievingly. 'You actually *know* Angela and you arranged with her that she would accept me if Abe set up the date? Then you inveigled Abe into making the actual suggestion to me? What the hell are you, Becky, a brothel madam?'

'I could get very angry at you for that crack, Simon,' Becky retorted hotly, 'but I won't. I'll be patient with you and explain.'

'That should make entertaining listening,' replied Simon, ashamed to note a sneer in his tone.

She went on briskly: 'Was Angela's flat

anything like a brothel?'

'I wouldn't know, I've never had any experience of brothels,' he replied, adding honestly: 'But it was a really nice place to be.'

'And was Angela like any common prostitute?'

'Again, I can't speak from experience, but I'd make a guess she was damned *un*common. She seems able to give a kind of love unstintingly — and I do mean love, not sex alone. She's about the kindest and most considerate girl I've ever known — whatever may be said of her morals.'

'Right,' said Becky, 'on that we're agreed. Now, to revert to those bad days when Abe took his pleasure where he could. I tolerated it while he was discreet, but unfortunately he became mixed up with a real slag who wasn't averse to making her 'lovers' known — if she thought she could get anything from it. I was able to bear it while the affairs remained secret, but that girl's boastings and tittle-tattle were like a slap in the face to me and I resolved to do something about it.

'At that time,' she continued, 'I was building up my own business connections in London and, partly due to the burblings of a business associate somewhat overdone on after-lunch brandy, I hit upon the idea of actually selecting a girl for Abe, setting her up in a flat and then arranging for her to 'pick him up' — but in a nice and delicate manner.'

'And it worked?' Simon marvelled.

'Admirably. The girl had her flat free and money to live on — businesses saw to the money side of the arrangement — and Abe was ever a generous man. She was good to him and good for him, and the best side-effect was that he and I actually seemed to draw closer together. But then the girl spoilt it all by getting greedy and taking in any old Tom, Dick or Harry, right, left and centre. It became necessary for me to collapse the whole set-up before anything serious happened. After a long time spent thinking it all out, I restructured the whole set-up — fresh flat, fresh girl, fresh arrangements, but in due course she too found a way of spoiling it and wound up paying protection money.

'My London business connections knew just how to 'warn off' those people and they did so, but by then the whole thing had soured and I dropped the scheme for a while, letting Abe make his own arrangements, which he did with considerably more discretion than before. But of course he was making it where he could and I favoured the 'controlled environment' principle.'

Simon marvelled at the woman's calm attitude to the whole business and yet still found it most difficult to believe what he was hearing. 'My God, Becky,' he objected, 'you sound almost clinical about it.'

'I can afford to be. All the evidence I possessed at that time showed that a satisfied Abe meant a good life here at home. In the end, though, I was obliged to face yet another fact of life — that a girl in that line of business will invariably seek other customers to fill the blank times between visits by her principal client. How, I wondered, could that be made acceptable? Then I had the solution. Why not select a sufficient number of regulars for her and hand-pick each one of them just as the girl herself would be hand-picked. She would then have full employment, a good income and home, and no temptation to seek outside liaisons. As an additional incentive to keep the girl to the selected clients she would be in no doubt that just one extra-curricular sortie would see her heaved out without notice. I got my plans into order and waited to find the girl. There have been a number since the decision was made — Angela is the most recent replacement.'

'So,' Simon observed harshly, 'Angela accommodates a syndicate!' He experienced a strange hurt feeling and his spirits fell accordingly. He was sure he would have much preferred to retain his own impressions.

'In a sense, yes, and she is intensely loyal to her commitment.'

'Yet she took me,' said Simon pointedly.

'A special arrangement. You needed

someone like her — kind and understanding — it was a very special thing.'

Sadly, Simon found himself wondering
just how special.

★ ★ ★

Abe Rousker breezed into the lounge of
his home where Simon sat alone. 'Becky
told me you were in here. How is it with
you?'

Simon nodded absently. 'I'm fine,' he
replied distantly. 'I got back from London
rather late this afternoon and I came
round in the hope of having a chat with
you.'

Abe cocked his head and frowned
cautioningly. 'About — you know — Or is
it a business matter?'

'Business.'

Abe turned towards the drinks cabinet.
'Sherry?' he asked over his shoulder.

'Please.'

When they had the glasses in their
hands Abe Rousker crossed the room and
sat in a chair opposite Simon. 'You'll stay
for a meal?' he invited. 'We can talk after.'

Simon shook his head. 'Becky has already offered,' he replied, 'but I really think I should get back to the office.'

Abe shrugged. 'As you wish, boy,' he said. 'Now — what can I do for you?'

'It's about Rachel Fuhrmann and my divorce,' Simon began slowly. 'Suppose my visit to her was a careful setup; suppose that private detective was already primed and planted; suppose someone stood to gain by framing me on an infidelity accusation. Who would that be?'

'We've been over all the ground before, Simon,' Abe reminded him sadly, 'and we've come up with no worthwhile conclusions. I realize how you must feel, my boy, but really all it amounts to is that Marion wanted a divorce so she put that detective onto your tail and he came up with a result. So he and everyone else concerned misinterpreted your reasons for being in Rachel's flat and Marion has got her divorce. So who cares? Does it really matter any more? You're better off without Marion anyway! Get yourself a real woman, one with enough love in her to surmount any difficulty.'

'Like your Becky?' Simon suggested dully.

Abe Rousker threw him an odd yet appraising glance. 'Yes,' he agreed with a deep sincerity, 'just like my Becky.'

Simon swallowed the last of his sherry and rose to leave. 'All the same,' he said, 'I'd be grateful if you'd keep your eyes and ears open for the remotest hint of anything which might indicate some less obvious reason for rigging that adultery thing.'

'It would be pointless,' Abe declared, rising and placing a fatherly arm about Simon's shoulders, 'but — for you — anything! You're like a son to us, you know that, Simon. Becky and I could refuse you nothing. Now, you're sure you won't stay and eat with us? It's strictly a non-kosher meal. You know us, lapsed beyond recovery. I'm sure it would please your gentile palate.'

Simon warmed in the glow of the man's friendship and some of the depression slipped away so that he was able to smile again. 'Thanks, Abe,' he replied. 'You're very kind, but I really must go — even if Becky's about to serve up a side of pork!'

* * *

Making his way back to the little side-street shop which served him as an office and — of recent months — a home, Simon found he was continually turning over in his mind the situation in which he now existed.

He was divorced and nominally free of Marion yet bound firmly to her because of the alimony and his continuing responsibility for their daughter Sarah. The payment of alimony he deeply resented but accepted that for men in his position the resentment was par for the course. The one small relief was that there were visiting rights with Sarah, but he knew that no matter how rigidly he adhered to the minimal visiting facilities, Marion would see to it that he was made to feel that he was intruding upon her, personally; and that despite any court ruling he had no rights other than those bestowed by Marion. Sadly he acknowledged that Sarah was soon to be drawn away from him.

In search of relief from his dejection, he thought pleasurably of his twenty-four hours with Angela Whitney, but consideration of her inevitably threw up recollections of that peculiar set-up as described by Becky Rousker. To his annoyance he found it tended to confuse his mental picture of the girl and detracted from the pleasure and comfort he had derived from her.

Did he object to her being a shared girl? He found that he did. It was all right until Becky put it into actual words. On the way up to London he had accepted that she had other men, and yet, however nervously, he had gone ahead. So far as he then cared she was some unknown call-girl, and despite having had no previous dealings with others of her kind he had felt no moral objections to using her services. In the event he had found her delightful and had thoroughly enjoyed her company, so why should he find anything disturbing in Becky's revelations?

He believed that Becky had tried to set him at ease when she made her explanations, but in that she had failed and Simon came to wonder exactly to what extent she had controlled the arrangements. It was this aspect which he now found objectionable. Simon felt that he had been manipulated rather than that he had taken advantage of the kind gesture of a friend. Of late, he had been manipulated enough.

At his office, he let himself in, threw off his coat and made a pot of tea. A few cream crackers and some cheese would then have to sustain him while he sat at the desk and applied himself to business.

It was some time later that he heard the front door-latch turn as someone tried to come in, and then there came a familiar rap on the glass panel. Simon opened the door, and Sarah came into his arms, clinging tightly to him while he hugged her and swung her round joyfully.

'Hello, Pop,' said Sarah, grinning cheerfully but failing to hide the hint of moisture in her eyes.

'Hello, love,' he returned delightedly.

'You couldn't be more welcome.' He set her down and closed the door. 'Come and sit down — I'll make some fresh tea.'

'Let me make it, Dad, please?' She peeled off her coat and revealed her Girl Guide uniform.

He smiled. 'Of course.'

Sarah was already taller than her mother and showed no sign that she would be other than slim like the women of Simon's family, but she had Marion's hair and eyes which were attractive when enhanced by the face of young innocence.

'Dad,' Sarah began cautiously from the direction of the cupboard upon which stood the office kettle, 'about that woman, Rachel Fuhrmann.'

'Put her out of your mind, love,' he urged kindly. 'It's all just a bad dream.'

'I don't believe you did sleep with her.'

Young innocence! Where was it now? He thought about it for a moment. Sarah was fourteen, going on fifteen, and kids — especially the girls — matured earlier these days and they understood about life.

'Thanks,' said Simon, trying to remain

matter-of-fact, 'you're one of a select few.'

'I'm not just playing the loyal daughter, Dad,' Sarah declared. 'It's simply not your scene.'

He chuckled wryly. 'Your mother must have thought differently. She was confident enough to put a private detective on my tail!'

'Mum?' Sarah sounded incredulous. 'Hire a detective?'

'Sure. The man who gave evidence at the hearing. His name was Wilkie. He's not a local man.'

'Mum didn't hire him,' said Sarah emphatically.

'Oh?' Simon intoned, clearly in doubt. 'I'm sure she didn't.'

Simon was caught in a cleft stick. He had no wish to involve the girl, her life would be difficult enough — pulled between her parents as she was — and yet he longed to know just why she was so confident that Wilkie had not been employed by her mother. And, if Marion had not set Wilkie after him, why had the man been there, observing Rachel Fuhrmann's flat at so opportune a moment and why would he pass on his information to Marion? For the first time Simon found he was willing to give serious consideration to the suggestion put forward by Angela.

His curiosity got the upper hand of his reluctance. 'What makes you so sure?'

'The man approached her, I'm certain of it.'

'At home?'

'No. No. I think it must have been at work because I can remember her coming home one day in a filthy temper and she was ranting on about your infidelity. She kept saying how fortunate it was that 'that man' had been on hand to see you going into that woman's flat. By the time you came home that day she'd got a grip on herself and she bottled it all up until she was ready to go ahead with the divorce. When she faced you with that announcement she'd been nurturing that piece of information for a long time. I think I shall remember *that* row all my life.'

'It's always the innocent bystander who gets hurt,' Simon philosophized unoriginally.

'I think Mum cheated you,' Sarah declared, ignoring his remark.

'You do?' Simon had the uncomfortable feeling that he was treading dangerous ground.

'Well, yes. I mean — not being a proper wife to you all those years.'

Embarrassed and a little angry, Simon slammed the palm of one hand on the desk. 'Now who on earth told you that?' he demanded.

'It was in the newspapers,' she returned simply. 'The reports of the divorce hearing. Apart from your denial of ever having been with that woman, it was your only defence.'

'Newspapers!' Simon snorted derisively.

'Mum told me, anyhow!'

'I can't pretend to find *that* believable,' he said chidingly.

'But it's true!' Sarah defended. 'I told her that I didn't believe you would waste your time on another woman while you had her to turn to. That was when she just sort of snapped out that she didn't encourage 'that sort of thing' and that it was certain that a weak man like you would look elsewhere.'

'Okay,' Simon accepted reluctantly, 'but I do wish she hadn't confided in you so. It's a heavy burden for one so young.'

Sarah poured two cups of tea and carried them across to her father's desk. 'I'm young,' she agreed, setting down the cups, 'but that doesn't mean I know nothing of these things and can't make some sort of balanced judgement.'

Simon smiled sadly but proudly. 'It seems my little girl is on the way to becoming an intelligent young woman,' he observed.

'Did Mum refuse you?'

'Yes,' he admitted.

'But you played fair.' She said it as a statement of fact.

'Yes. And that's no lie. I stuck to the rules all right — but don't imagine I wasn't tempted!'

'You'd hardly be human if you weren't.'

Simon found the girl's calm acceptance of facts almost unnerving, so much so that he found he had to try to let the matter drop. He drank some of the tea, made an appreciative face and went back to sorting through file cards.

For a few moments Sarah watched in silence. Then: 'Playing patience?' she asked lightly.

'Looking for clues.'

'You're on a case?'

He shrugged, smiled fleetingly and explained briefly, 'One of my own.'

'Oh? And what are you looking for?'

'A common denominator.'

'For what?'

'To tie that detective, Wilkie, to Rachel Fuhrmann and to me. I know why *I* had business with Rachel, but what was *his* business with her? If I can find the answer to that one I may be able to sort out this lousy game.'

'So you already suspected,' Sarah observed. 'What I've told you didn't really help.'

'It helped,' he assured her. 'It confirmed a line of thought.'

'How do you go about looking for this common denominator?' Sarah asked.

'I was doing an investigation for a firm,' Simon began.

'Which firm?'

He smiled apologetically. 'I'm sorry, love, but my business really is confidential.'

Sarah returned his smile. 'Of course,' she agreed. 'I shouldn't have asked.'

'The investigation,' Simon continued, 'took me to Rachel Fuhrmann. Something took Wilkie to Rachel Fuhrmann. Now if I can find in my files any point where my cross-references indicate some other line leading to Rachel, it's a pretty good chance that is the one Wilkie was following.'

'How do you check the cross-references?'

'I keep pretty full records of most local businesses,' Simon explained, 'that's how I'm able to check commercial credit-worthiness, and I have good coverage of out-of-town businesses with local connections. Of course, they're all coded to maintain confidentiality, but tracing code-words to common points can go a long way to easing the job.'

'With all these cards?' Sarah cried, appalled. 'Good gracious, Dad, that must be like doing a year's pools coupons at one sitting and while wearing a blindfold!'

Simon chuckled. 'Something of that order,' he agreed, 'and with the same slender chance of success.'

'What happened to your desk-top computer?' she demanded. 'This is the perfect job for it!'

'That had to go when things started to blow up in my face,' Simon explained ruefully.

'But you *need* a computer!'

'Don't I know it! The trouble is that they cost money and I can't keep up the rental payments now.'

'You should get to know Miss Rhodes,' Sarah said out of the blue.

'Miss Rhodes?'

'My second-year form mistress — you must remember her.'

'So how does that affect me?'

'Really, Dad, you must be miles away. We've agreed you really need a computer for the job you've got on here! She has strong links with a computer company, she knows how to buy computer time and how best to use it!'

'Wonderful,' he scoffed, 'and how do I persuade her to involve herself in solving my problems?'

'She's single, Dad. A spinster, nearly thirty years old and not a man in sight! There must still be *some* life left in you, isn't there? In any case, you need a woman about this place!'

Sarah chuckled triumphantly, kissed her father lightly and, in another moment, was gone.

# 4

Elaine Rhodes experienced an almost girlish tremble of excited anticipation in the pit of her stomach. This was the moment her most wishful dreams had sought for her as a starting-point for a journey into romance. And Elaine was an incurable romantic, self-confessed, and totally at odds with her workaday occupation teaching growing girls to use mathematics and computers as weapons in the battle of life. She knew that unless the longed-for miracle occurred she would be faced with a life of virtual loneliness because she had so few real friends — a shortage due to a chronic shyness which unfortunately manifest itself in sharp-tongued rebuff of extended hands of friendship. She was painfully aware of this shortcoming and longed to overcome it, but seemed unable to find the way. In the event, this habit of curt defence persisted.

Then there had come a man. He was married and the father of one of the girls in her form a year or so ago. Simon Shelley had come to her to explain his daughter's absence from school because of a broken leg, Elaine could remember the moment as clearly as though it were but yesterday.

He had approached her with a shy, disarming smile, his eyes quickly appraising her face, hair, figure and legs. At once this visual summarizing had caused that hideous shyness to rear up, triggering the acid-tongued response to his greeting.

Generally it had been Elaine's experience that people recoiled from the whiplash words as though stung, but Simon had boldly stood his ground. With patience and calm he had answered her questions and parried her sallies so that their cutting edge was blunted. He had seemed unusually well practised at the art, and she could recall how she had wondered about that.

The effect upon her was to make him the object of her dreams — waking or sleeping.

Only this morning, Sarah Shelley had approached her during break-time and, after a brief recapitulation on computers, had hinted broadly at her father's business problems and his current lack of computer facilities.

'It's a matter of finding a common denominator,' Sarah had explained, 'but with facts rather than figures. I suggested feeding the facts into a computer, but he can no longer afford to lease a small computer. Then I suggested he should ask you about ways of renting computer time. I thought you would be able to advise him — but I think he was a bit shy about it and rather afraid that he'd be imposing.'

Elaine had felt her pulse-rate quicken, and she had thought quickly on how best to take advantage of this heaven-sent opportunity. 'Perhaps you should give me a little time to work out something. I may be able to advise you and then you can pass it on to your father.'

'Oh.'

Had Elaine been mistaken or had Sarah's tone really slumped?

'I was hoping — '

Yes, there certainly had been a note of disappointment, but the girl had accepted the situation with notable reluctance, and Elaine found herself wondering about that.

Why was Sarah so disappointed? Had she merely been trying to help her father or had there been something more? Could Sarah have been trying to tell her something?

It had been at that point that Elaine's romanticism had cut into the logical thought processes. Suppose Sarah had really been saying that she wouldn't mind if she, Elaine Rhodes, set her cap at Simon Shelley. The more she considered this notion, the more Elaine liked it. With a new pleasure she recalled the way he had appraised her and the fact that she had seen only approval in his eyes. Of course, she had to admit to herself that it could well be wishful thinking. Would Sarah really find her acceptable as a partner for her father and, if so, how far would she go to promote a courtship?

Elaine remembered with some concern

that when Sarah had been a second-year student, and she her form mistress, they had clashed pretty dramatically more times than enough, and she was willing to concede that much of the fault for that lay at her own door. Yet things had changed and the change seemed to have begun with Simon's visit to explain about his daughter's fractured leg. Elaine had mellowed very rapidly — and not only towards Sarah — thereafter.

She had seen little enough of him but had clasped to her bosom some dramatically erotic romantic notions about him. She and Sarah had first begun to understand each other. From that had stemmed mutual respect and, in its turn, liking. It was just possible that Sarah could see her as a replacement for her mother — perhaps not as a mother but at least as a wife for her father.

Elaine's soliloquy ended in a telephone kiosk. She picked up the telephone, dialled, panicked and rang off again before the connection could be made. Taking a firm grip on her nerves she dialled again and heard the 'phone ringing at the other end. The telephone was lifted and a man's voice — soft, husky and a little tired — repeated the number and added: 'Simon Shelley — 'Information'.'

Swallowing an odd feeling in her throat, Elaine forced herself to speak clearly. 'This is Elaine Rhodes.' She felt sure he must notice the nervous quiver in her voice, and she wished fervently that the ground would open up and swallow her.

'Miss Rhodes? Sarah's teacher?'

'One of them,' she qualified. 'Yes.'

'What can I do for you, Miss Rhodes?' he asked, a note of concern colouring his words. 'Nothing's wrong with Sarah, I hope?'

Elaine drew a deep breath and gripped the handset grimly. 'Oh, no,' she hastened to reassure him and to get her piece said before her nerve failed again. 'Sarah's fine. We were speaking this morning, she and I, on the use of computers in business and your daughter mentioned that you had a problem ideally suited to computer solution. She said you could no longer afford your own computer but were interested in renting computer time.' There, it was said. Exciting but quite painless.

'Well,' he began, and hesitated.

'She was wrong to discuss it with me?' Elaine suggested.

'Oh, no.' Simon's accompanying chuckle struck into her left ear and brought instant relief of her fears. 'Perhaps she may have jumped the gun a little, but that's all. You know: 'Stir up the old Dad and get him started in the right direction'.'

'If you would like some help and advice,' Elaine offered with a false casualness, 'I could call in at your office.'

'I'd appreciate that,' Simon replied.

'This afternoon, if you wish. Say between four and half-past?'

'I have to go out this afternoon,' Simon returned cautiously. 'I should be back by that time, but it's by no means certain and I'd hate to inconvenience you when you are being so kind.'

'Of course,' said Elaine understand-ingly. 'I realize you have your living to earn and your hours must be extremely variable. Suppose I get to your office as soon as I can and hang on until, say, five?'

'Won't this interfere with your meal arrangements?'

'I can still get home in ample time.'

'Very well then,' Simon agreed. 'I accept your kind offer and look forward to seeing you soon after four.'

Elaine stepped from the telephone box quite sure her trembling knees would give way and deposit her, full length, on the pavement.

★   ★   ★

Simon set the telephone back on its cradle, lit a cigar and indulged in a whimsical smile. His Sarah, he considered, was a clever little minx. Knowing that he would never bother to ask the Rhodes woman for assistance, she had contrived to reverse the order of things and have the teacher open contact — a gesture he could hardly refuse point-blank.

He didn't much care whether he could

gain anything by using his meagre funds to buy computer time but he wouldn't let Sarah down, nor would he make Miss Rhodes feel foolish. He tried to recall the woman.

She would be in her late twenties by now; she was of medium build and height and her figure was pretty good if a trifle on the plump side; pleasant enough once he'd got into conversation with her; she smiled rarely, and then shyly. Her most notable features were her red-tinged fair hair and a complexion devoid of the pastiness so common with redheads. And, now that he thought about them, she had good legs.

Simon wondered that Sarah had summoned up enough nerve to broach the matter to the woman and that Miss Rhodes had deigned to offer help. He shook his head and chuckled at the turn of events, then went out to get lunch before going in search of Rachel Fuhrmann.

He pressed the bell-push beside the door of Rachel's flat, and she opened it promptly enough. 'Simon! This *is* a surprise! You're about the last person I would have expected to call. Do come in.' She carried only a slight trace of the accents of her native Germany, her voice was cultured, her tone bordered on the supercilious and her general presence was that of an actress with inflated ideas of her capability and importance.

Following her into the flat, Simon pressed his back against the door to close it while he continued watching Rachel. She was tall and slim, elegant; dark haired and dark eyed; and she was undeniably attractive.

Rachel, never the one to give a poor performance even at short notice, turned in one flowing movement and sat on the settee, her legs crossed and showing much of their elegant length where the housecoat gaped open. 'What can I do for you, darling?'

Simon was impressed, no man worth his salt could fail to be impressed, but he had seen it all before. Rachel's opening gambit had changed not at all.

'For starters you can tell me how Wilkie came to fix me so easily,' Simon suggested, giving her a cigarette and lighting one for himself.

'I'd have thought you would have given up worry about that little business,' she pouted. 'At one time I was convinced you actually looked forward to having your freedom.'

'About Wilkie,' Simon pursued resolutely.

'Suppose I put him onto you? Suppose I wanted you for myself?'

'Now the truth.'

'Darling,' Rachel chided. 'Would I lie to you?'

'To God's face, if the mood was on you.'

She dropped the bantering tone. 'Really, Simon, wherever is your tact? If you want my co-operation you're going about it in a very funny way.'

'Stuff the funnies *and* the waffle,' Simon snapped. 'Tell me about Wilkie!'

'What's it worth to me?'

'My promise not to broadcast certain of your activities to certain people.'

'Blackmail!'

Simon shrugged. 'This has been a dirty

fight, so I'll fight dirty now.'

Rachel sneered openly. 'You can't get to me that way, Simon, you should know that. It's a fact of life that my activities are pretty well known hereabouts. Wake up to reality, Simon, you did have the good sense not to try calling me as a witness in your defence — recognize facts — my sexual life means nothing!'

'Oh, I wasn't thinking of *that*,' Simon assured her calmly. 'There are quite a few people who'd be very upset if certain of your shareholdings became public knowledge.'

'Really, Simon,' Rachel protested, 'you are quite unprincipled.' She smiled almost approvingly. 'A man after my own heart.'

'Wilkie,' he persisted.

'I don't know — and that's straight.'

Simon found himself believing her despite all his knowledge of her. 'Okay,' he acknowledged. 'You don't know for a fact, but what do you know that you are *not* so aware of?'

'Hmm?' Rachel's rising inflexion proclaimed her puzzlement.

'Someone,' Simon said emphatically, 'doesn't trust you. I don't know the exact reason, mind, but they set Wilkie to keep an eye on you. He saw me here and decided to try to make a bit of cash on the side by shopping me to Marion. But that's by the way — the real question is this: Who would set a watch on you?'

'Darling — really! How many men have jealous wives? Why don't you ask this Wilkie fellow direct?'

'Come to, Rachel. Wilkie's a professional and he's not about to divulge the names of any of his clients. There has to be another way for me to find out and you're it! There has to be a tie-up somewhere and you have to be a key figure in some funny business or other — important enough to make it worth while to pay Wilkie to watch you and everyone who called on you.'

Rachel sighed and stretched languorously, revealing the 'X' certificate areas of her sleek body. She was completely unconcerned that the open housecoat left nothing of note concealed, and Simon found that he was unmoved either to disgust or excitement. He never had fancied Rachel as a bed-mate, and that was another possible reason he objected to having his name linked with hers in the divorce court.

'And what,' she asked wearily, 'could I have been up to that would make me so important?'

'That,' Simon returned flatly, nodding at the fleshy revelation.

'You find me distracting?' There was a challenge in her tone.

'Not at all. I just wonder if that body of yours may have got you into something deeper than you supposed.'

'Such as?' Rachel flipped the housecoat across the view with an irritable gesture. It was the first real sign Simon had seen that he was getting to the woman.

'I don't know yet, but I will, believe me — with or without your willing help. Frankly, if I were in your shoes I wouldn't fancy the situation one little bit. Someone has had a business fiddle going and you're involved somewhere along the line. You can bet they won't trust you. Aside from your apparently loose tongue and tendency to boast of 'conquests', you're far too ready to seize the main chance. They'll keep a close eye on you. Tell me: Who're your connections? Let me get to them before they get to you!'

'You have already pointed out to me, darling,' returned Rachel, recovering her composure, 'that Wilkie would tell you nothing because he's a professional. Well, allow me to say that I, too, am a professional. It's just not your lucky day. Don't try putting the frighteners on me, I don't scare all that easily. If there was a business risk it was more likely you than me so look to your own affairs and, in the meantime, get off my back!'

'You're a fool, Rachel,' Simon asserted.

'But not *that* kind of fool,' she retorted fiercely. 'Now, get out of here and stay out!'

⋆ ⋆ ⋆

Simon paused on the steps of the block of flats in which Rachel Fuhrmann lived and sniffed at the salt-laden air pushed along the street by the onshore wind. His slow study of the street scene before him took in a café which bore an Italian name and which was run by third-generation British citizens whose Italian, when spoken in Italy, branded them 'Englishmen'.

He checked his watch and saw that it was a little after 3 p.m. There was time to spare so he crossed the street to the café, ordered coffee and carried it to a table near the door. The coffee was good, but he took little pleasure from it as he reflected on the badly conducted interview with Rachel and his notable lack of success.

Rachel's eyes and her one irritable gesture — had they inadvertently told him something or did she offer a genuine clue somewhere amid the verbiage.

He felt there must be enough clues within easy grasp, probably within his own files — if only he could get them out. It was as likely as not that two cunning business brains had got together in some unholy alliance for the mutual benefit of their bank accounts. They would need to be on good terms of trust with each other, too, so maybe he could trace some previous collaboration.

Simon mulled over the idea, accepting it as no more than a point of debate and knowing it could as easily run him up a blind alley as along the right road.

The collaboration idea, however, could not in itself account for anyone wishing to pull him out of the picture by distracting him with the threat of divorce unless, of course, the collaboration was itself unexpected. What, he wondered, if two men who were normally daggers-drawn had seen an enterprise with sufficient prospect of reward to justify a suspension of hostilities?

A joint venture by such men would cause raised eyebrows and many questions if it became general knowledge, and they would probably be willing to go to considerable lengths to avoid discovery too soon.

The more he juggled with the notion, the better Simon liked it as a starting-point. The collaborators would be unlikely to trust each other implicitly and might well set a detective or detectives to keep an eye on things.

When the coffee was gone, Simon wandered back to his office deep in thought but getting nowhere. He sat down and set to work on the file cards with the holes punched all round the sides just a fraction of an inch in from the edge. Each hole represented a piece of standard information and by clipping out the edge of each relevant hole he could effectively record a basic fact. He selected his first pile of cards, thrust a steel needle through a hole and shook the stack gently. The cards which fell out were the first stage in narrowing the field of enquiry.

It was a small start and, with a heavy sigh, Simon began the long search, but he found it difficult to take an interest in the boring task of sorting out the first pile of cards before him, and Elaine Rhodes' arrival at four-fifteen brought the effort to an end.

Simon admitted her to his office and to the opportunity of checking his memory of her. She was solidly built and would always be so, but never fat. The rest of her was much as he had recalled earlier, but her smile was pleasant and came more readily, though there was an air of nervousness about it as she looked the part of the older single woman entering the lair of the single predatory male.

Simon was highly amused.

# 5

Angela replaced the telephone on the coin-box cradle, picked up her small suitcase and vanity-case and stepped away from the telephone hood set against the wall of the gloomy concourse of Beverington Central Station. She walked across to the waiting-room, went inside, sat down and fumbled nervously in her handbag for a cigarette. Her fingers trembled badly and dropped the lighter into her lap, she retrieved it and lit the cigarette on the second try.

She marvelled at the degree of her own nervousness — and she a woman of the world. Of the world? Or a surprisingly narrow section of it? She became aware of a lack of the right kind of experience to cope with her present position. It was a position of her own creation and she need not have been there. The trouble had been the unaccustomed sense of loneliness which had gnawed away her usual calm, and she had run towards Simon Shelley.

Simon could relax her and make her feel wanted for herself even though sex had figured largely in their brief encounter. Angela drew on a cigarette and wished for him to come quickly. The cigarette was doing no good for her, she dropped it onto the littered floor and crushed it out, then pulled her coat more tightly about her to try to keep out the chill of isolation and to offer herself some imagined comfort.

She saw him through the grubby windows of the waiting-room as he strode purposefully across the concourse. He looked tall, assured, strong and dependable. Angela stood up and turned to face him as he entered, her nervous eyes searched his face for even the smallest signs of anger or displeasure, but saw none.

Angela smiled cautiously. 'Mohammed,' she said, 'has come to the mountain.'

'And the mountain is duly impressed,' Simon returned, smiling reassuringly as he took her into his arms and kissed her hard.

Angela returned the kiss with every ounce of her being, revelling in the pure pleasure and relief of once again being with him, and as the kiss ended she was able to relax against his warm body with a sense of homecoming she had never before known.

'Walk or taxi?' Simon asked.

'How far?'

'Ten minutes on foot.'

'A taxi, please, there's something I must do as quickly as possible.'

'Right,' Simon agreed briskly, picking up her cases. 'Outside on the double! A carriage awaits.'

Angela chuckled happily and followed him to the taxi rank where they entered the leading cab and were driven to his office.

Simon guided Angela through the office and up to his flat where he waved an arm towards one of the doors. 'Bathroom,' he said, bearing in mind the note of urgency in her voice when she decided on a taxi.

She turned into his arms, her own arms about his neck and her lips searching his face for fresh places to kiss.

'I thought — ' he began as her tears wet his cheeks and left the flavour of salt on his lips.

'This was what I needed,' she breathed contentedly. 'To be with you again is all I wished. I just had to come; the flat became a prison cell.' Angela clung to him fiercely. 'Do you mind too much?'

'My God, no,' he returned, crushing her against him, 'but I'd have been angry if I'd known you'd sat alone in your flat, feeling as you do, and not come down here to me. The very least I can do is be company — and I'm sure I can manage something better than that.'

For a time they stood in the middle of the living-room, clasped in each other's arms and basking in a special warmth.

Angela was the first to break the silence. 'That woman,' she asked cautiously, 'did she come?'

'Yes — and went,' he replied. 'Did you by any chance come down here because of her?'

'I came because of you. Look, Simon, I'm confused about some things — I want to try to explain them to you but I don't know how. I suppose I'm feeling vulnerable and the thought of — Am I being proprietorial?'

'Just vulnerable,' he whispered softly as he kissed her left ear.

Angela quivered under his touch. 'I really did come just because I need to be with you.' She knew she was saying it badly but she was so uncertain of herself that the right words would not come or, if they were there in her mind, she hadn't the courage to voice them.

Simon held her away at arm's length where he could more easily study her face and reddened eyes. He smiled seriously. 'You realize what it is you're afraid to say, don't you?' he said earnestly.

At last it came. 'That I love you?' she breathed wonderingly. 'That I'm *in* love with you? I'm told there's a difference, but I'm afraid it escapes me and I've no idea which to acknowledge or if I should admit to either. All I know is that I couldn't bear another moment without at least seeing you. Is that enough for me to say until I can judge for myself? At least I know that what I was giving my friends was affection and not love. You have taken me into a new world that I don't understand.'

Drawing her close again he kissed her earnestly and then whispered in her ear. 'You must know I face a similar dilemma.'

'I think I know,' Angela agreed, 'but I do allow myself hope even though a girl in my position — '

'You're as entitled to love and to be loved as anyone else. My trouble is that I've been over the course once and I'm not sure just how reliable my instincts are. It could take time before I know.'

'Then I shall wait. It won't be easy but it can be done, it will *have* to be done.'

Simon helped her out of her coat and led her to the bedroom. 'You can probably find room for your things in the bottom drawer of the chest,' he suggested. 'Get yourself settled in while I get some supper for you.'

'A cup of tea,' Angela assured him,

smiling, 'would make me your slave forever.'

He scampered to the door. 'Let me at that kettle,' he growled.

Angela chuckled. 'But nothing to eat for me, if you don't mind,' she said. 'Tomorrow I shall fix *you* something.'

Simon smiled understandingly. He winked. 'Sure enough,' he agreed.

In the kitchen, away from Angela's view, Simon's face and attitude changed dramatically as he looked inward at himself and admitted to a powerful urge to run back to the girl and tell her that he needed her and loved her. And he cursed himself for lacking the courage to do so in the face of memories of his failure with Marion.

★　★　★

Elaine Rhodes strove to give calm consideration of her position. Simon Shelley had been polite, welcoming and really hopeful that she might be helpful to him, but there had been nothing more. She realized that her girlish romanticism had cast him in the rôle of an eager lover whereas she needed to be more realistic and practical in seeking ways to show him that she would make a suitable mate.

The apparent purpose of her visit to him had proved abortive. Sarah's idea that buying computer time would help her father had been soundly based, but his strict adherence to his coding and the demand for confidentiality had made the proposal impractical. In the preparation and programing stages she would have had to know more precisely what his business was about, and Simon, for all his understanding and kindness, had been unable to bring himself to break the wall of confidentiality.

'You've scarcely done justice to your dinner, Elaine,' Clair Rhodes chided gently.

Elaine looked at her across the table, seeing her mother vaguely through eyes and mind seeking to orientate her in time, place and company.

'You seem so far away,' her father added solicitously. 'Are you sure you're all right?'

Elaine moved her hand in a gesture indicative of nothing pertinent. 'Computer problems,' she replied, hoping the words would suffice.

They did not.

'Computers!' her father snorted good naturedly. 'They're little better than animals — feed them right and they'll treat you right. The trouble is people! They feed the electronic animal the things which please themselves, and served in their own way, and just as often they feed the animal wrongly. It survives, of course, and appears healthy — but, one day — ' He made a throat-cutting gesture with the edge of his hand.

'This is a problem of encoding a code,' Elaine replied absently, her thoughts on Simon's warm smile, 'not one of information.'

'No doubt the code to which you refer contains information?'

'Yes.'

'And you do not know what that information is?'

'No.'

'I take it, then, that it is supplied by a third party?'

'Yes.'

'Then you cannot judge its accuracy or, for that matter, any other factor connected with it so how can you be sure that you are feeding your 'animal' correctly? It follows, therefore, that you will be quite unable to check the veracity of the results,' Henry Rhodes concluded on a note of triumph. He was not a vindictive man within his family circle but he did enjoy teasing his daughter about 'her' computers.

Elaine, for her part, accepted in the right vein. Her father, she knew from experience, had an acute mind where business and financial matters were concerned, he was very fond of indicating errors in computerized accounts submitted to him by businesses both private and public — and he had never been wrong so far.

'The question of accuracy, in that context, doesn't arise for me in this matter,' she replied. 'So long as what is on the file-cards can be accurately interpreted for the computer, my concern ends right there. The accuracy of the information and the efficacy of the computer's response to questions is entirely the customer's worry.'

'Customer?' Henry pounced like a cat upon a mouse.

Elaine shrugged. 'A figure of speech,' she said.

Rhodes persisted. 'I thought, perhaps, that this project might be extra-curricular.'

'It is.'

'So you *do* have a customer, then.'

'No, but one of the computer businesses will have a customer if I can crack this problem.'

'Who is your 'customer'?' Henry pressed.

'Really, Henry,' Clair Rhodes cut in chidingly, 'do stop harassing the girl. Her mind must be in enough of a tangle with all that electronic jargon!'

'Bosh!' snorted Henry. 'Elaine has a clear sharp mind, she can cope!'

But Elaine was far less certain of the clarity of her mind. Her thoughts seemed to be milling in frantic pandemonium, and the turmoil could all be traced back to her visit to Simon Shelley.

Henry, not in the least deterred by his wife, continued his pursuit of an answer. 'Who is this fellow, anyway?'

'The father of one of my pupils,' Elaine replied offhandedly, 'Sarah Shelley.'

The change in her father was sudden and violent — a sleeping tiger kicked into wakefulness. 'Simon Shelley?' he demanded, red with rage. 'The man's a rogue, a trickster and a divorcé.'

Mother and daughter stared open-mouthed at this man who never exploded in anger.

'Really! Henry!' Clair Rhodes protested.

'Dad!' Elaine added in harmony.

'Young woman,' Henry snapped, brushing aside the objections, 'you will break all connection with that man — at once!'

'But why?' Elaine was too astonished at the outburst and the outrageous demand to be able to say more.

'I've given sufficient reason,' Henry returned curtly.

Elaine felt the colour rise to her cheeks and with it rose an anger so fierce as to startle her with its strength. Her eyes flashed bright sparks and her jaw set hard.

'Your so-called reasons,' she snapped back, 'are vague and unsubstantiated. If you imagine you can *order* me not to assist Mr Shelley, I advise you to think again! Indeed, even a civil request would require sounder reasons than you appear able to give!'

Henry's anger flared even higher. Never had his daughter addressed him in so rude a manner. It was another manifestation of the evil influence of Simon Shelley, it must be. He had polluted her mind and destroyed her meek obedience to his guiding hand.

'I *forbid* you to see him again!' he roared.

'Forbid?' Elaine's face suddenly drained white and her raised voice fell away to a soft and throaty sound bearing more menace than all the shouting. 'Forbid?' she repeated intensely. 'And who d'you think you are to forbid me anything? I'm a woman of twenty-seven, educated, intelligent, emancipated. I may live under your roof and accept that your rules and wishes weigh heavily in this house, but I will not accept *orders*, nor will I permit you to dictate with whom I shall associate!'

She rose and turned away from the table, agonizingly aware of the wounded and puzzled look on the face of her mother and the storm playing across her father's facial muscles.

'Then,' snarled Henry, 'you shall leave my house!'

'Henry!' Clair wailed.

★　★　★

Angela Whitney awoke in Simon's bed, it was dark, but she could feel him there. She moved her body against his, luxuriating in his nearness and his arms holding her secure. Never had she seen herself as a one-man woman and still she could not do so entirely, the habit of several men was too deeply ingrained, but at least she could dwell upon the sense of belonging;

of certain advantages in a feeling of permanence — even of monogamy.

The bedside clock told her it was 4 a.m., and she reflected upon how easily it might have been 4 a.m. in the total loneliness of her flat.

She kissed Simon's chest, felt his arms squeeze her reassuringly and relax.

'I could change,' she murmured. 'I could give it up.'

'Your job? You're a professional, you'd not find it easy,' Simon cautioned softly.

'But I *could* do it.'

'For whom?' he posed thoughtfully.

'For you.'

'No good,' he said, 'it doesn't work that way.'

'What way does it work?' Angela challenged.

He shrugged. 'People have to accept one another as they are. Change made for the wrong reason is destructive.'

'Could you accept me as I am?'

'I believe I could. I believe I already have to a great extent, but how can we be sure? I'm still in a flat spin from the furore of the divorce. To me, you're beautiful, you're honest and you ring as true as a bell. At this moment I believe I could accept anything, but how would it be if, say, we were married?'

Angela sighed. 'Sooner or later,' she pointed out, 'I shall have to retire anyway.'

'Like a professional footballer?'

'I suppose that's a fair analogy,' Angela agreed. 'His useful life is just as limited by age considerations if nothing else. The secret, as I see it, is in recognizing the right moment to retire.'

'I've seen pro footballers,' mused Simon, 'who felt so sure there was another good season in them that they held on too long, being transferred to lower and lower grades of football until they faded, penniless, from the scene.'

'Don't some go into business?' she asked.

'Some,' he acknowledged, 'but they generally have some qualification — what are you qualified for?'

'And some of them go amateur and do another job in the week,' Angela reminded him while quietly avoiding an answer to his question.

'Some, but they need a permit, a licence as it were, to play the amateur game.'

'A wife, I suppose, must count as an amateur,' Angela suggested. 'Within the marriage she's paid for nothing.'

Simon chuckled at the logic of it. 'That's true enough,' he conceded. 'No wages, only housekeeping and pin-money. I suppose the marriage certificate must constitute her 'amateur permit'.'

Angela smiled and allowed the conversation to lapse. After a time she drifted off into sleep and dreamt wonderful dreams of what might be.

\* \* \*

Elaine Rhodes awoke with a start, wondering why she had so abruptly snapped out of her sleep. She heard feet crunch softly on the gravel path at the back of the house, and she slipped from her bed and hurried to the window. It was first light and she could see her father passing down the garden path and behind the shed at the far end. When next he came into view he was just a vague figure making his way up the grassy knoll and into the trees.

She turned, intending to go back to bed, but her attention was caught and held by her reflection in the long mirror on the wardrobe door. She thought she looked good even to her own rather critical eye, but was that enough? On an impulse she reached down, took hold of the hem of her nightdress and drew the flimsy garment off over her head.

Once again she studied her reflection in the mirror. She was not slender but nor was she fat, her body was smoothly curved and firm-fleshed, her legs were shapely and her breasts were full and firm. Yes, it was quite good enough to have got her bedded on pure impulse — if her sharp-tongued defensive reactions had not killed, stone dead, the embryo desires of the few men in her life.

In her sleep she often dreamed. Erotic fantasies, often enough, and over the past few years Simon Shelley had featured in them all. Now, her reflection rekindled memories of those dreams and she felt her body respond with a deliciously exciting tingle.

Suddenly she saddened and her shoulders slumped so that only her breasts maintained their in-built pride. Wanting Simon so desperately was one thing, getting him was quite another. She drew the nightdress over her head and completed her journey back to bed.

Elaine tried desperately to turn away from thoughts of Simon Shelley, but all that would fill the space were thoughts of her father. Had he been serious when he declared: 'Then you shall leave my house!'? Was this early morning walk onto the neighbouring hillside any indication that he was, perhaps, having second thoughts? Whenever he had some serious problem on his mind it was quite usual for him to take that same walk and mull over the question.

Suppose she found herself in a position where she felt obliged to leave — whether by her father's edict or of her own volition. What would then become of her mother? Clair could barely have a year of her life left to her. The specialists had insisted that she need not be told and that she could be left to continue to run her home in blissful ignorance until her natural end which, they felt sure, would be sudden and without suffering.

Operations had been discussed and rejected as pointless, and Clair had been left to continue as normal a life as possible. She could manage well enough. Elaine now saw her father as a fresh problem — if she was obliged to leave home how would he react when his wife died? It was conceivable that he would hold Elaine partly to blame and might not, even in those circumstances, allow her home to help and offer comfort.

Elaine resolved with a marked reluctance at least to appear to go along with her father's wishes by steering clear of Simon for a while but, in the meantime, learn as much of him as possible.

As for actually catching the man when the time came for it, she began examining her assets. Her reflection had told her that she had the necessary sexual attractions but she was a virgin and totally inexperienced in their employment. She knew, too, that any sort of flirting on her part would appear gauche, and she had no wish to seem a giggling fool — nor had she any desire to appear sophisticated, such a façade would be impossible to support for any appreciable time.

She lay awake for a long time sampling this notion and that but coming to no firm conclusion until, in the end, she drifted off into a fitful doze.

*  *  *

Henry Rhodes trod the worn path up the low hill behind his house, deeply concerned about the atmosphere created in his home by his sudden and, to his wife and daughter, inexplicable outburst against Simon Shelley. Clair was upset and apprehensive; Elaine antagonized and under an ill-considered threat of eviction. He knew that the entire blame lay squarely upon his shoulders. His ranting against Simon Shelley had been a reflex defensive action sparked by an unreasoning fear that Elaine's association with the man might somehow adversely affect his own relationship with Marion Shelley.

What was worse, Elaine might stumble upon the truth that before her mother had gone to her grave her father had selected and was wooing her successor — at that a woman very little older than Elaine herself.

He felt that he would be perfectly justified in using every reasonable means for seeking to divert his daughter from Shelley, but he had to acknowledge that his first effort had been precipitate and ill-considered.

Henry turned his mind to Simon Shelley, unconsciously calling upon the old military adage 'Know your enemy'. Shelley had some sort of status or business enquiry agency which he ran primarily to give an economical service to local business people. No one, Henry was forced to admit in all honesty, had ever considered him a villain or a licentious person. Only Marion spoke badly of him, but then she had only a marital axe to grind.

He even found himself wondering

about the private detective, Stan Wilkie, who had given evidence for Marion. The man had enjoyed an easy passage; Simon Shelley's counsel had soft-pedalled the whole piece of evidence relating to Rachel Fuhrmann, but the woman's reputation was too well known for sleeping around and out it had come.

Henry found he wasn't really convinced that Shelley had slept with Rachel but that he needed to convince Elaine the man had, and for that he needed much better evidence than that trotted out in court.

In the end, he turned upon his heel and strode back to the house resolved upon two courses — first, to make his peace with Elaine and, second, to try to employ Wilkie to turn up more evidence detrimental to Shelley.

# 6

Simon watched the train draw away eastward on the start of its run to London. Angela's hand was just one of several waving from a window and he could no longer be sure which was hers. He gave a wide sweep of his arm in farewell and turned away, reluctant to return to earth and face life as it would now be in her absence.

He believed his growing affection for her was reaching beyond the bounds of reason; love was such an impossible thing to string between them and yet he permitted himself the luxury of admitting that he loved her and was torn by the parting. Angela was on her way back to a world where 'love' was a key word but a non-existence emotion, and he was returning to one where a little love was needed.

While his thoughts still dwelt on Angela, he indulged an impulse and rang

Abe Rousker's office to be told by a secretary that 'Mr Rousker is in 'Town' on business' and could she take a message?

Simon thanked her but said no, he would leave no message. The woman's reply had told him enough. It would probably be Abe who shared Angela's bed that night. He begrudged Abe nothing but would have preferred that the man with Angela be himself. Simon grinned wryly to himself as he stepped from the telephone booth. If he was jealous it was a singularly stupid emotion to entertain in the circumstances.

There was a tobacconist's shop on the station, and Simon stopped there long enough to buy a cigar which he smoked on his way back to the office where he gave his attention to a request from an out-of-town enquiry agency on behalf of their client, Peterfurn Limited, a furniture manufacturing company. They were requesting information on Beaver, a wholesale furniture business in Beverington.

Simon, despite his careful information-gathering, had never before heard of

Beavers, and this gap in his knowledge acted as a spur, turning his attention away from other jobs.

The address given by the agency included the name of a back lane which, to the best of his understanding, contained no address — private or business. Simon left his office again and walked the two hundred yards to the lane. He entered its western end, noting the bare rear walls of warehouses on his left and the backyards of Victorian terraced houses on his right. The houses were, he knew, for the most part, used as offices and the remaining few as flats and flatlets. None could properly lay claim to an address on the lane. The warehouses had their official addresses in the service road to the north, running parallel to the lane along which he walked.

Simon strolled along the lane making a slow and careful appraisal of what he would have considered familiar territory until this enquiry was tossed into his lap. He was on the point of considering 'Beaver' was cover for some sort of confidence trick when he found the tiny doorway with its plaque bearing the legend: Beaver (Wholesale) Ltd., Regd. Office.

The door itself was in a pretty poor condition and was certainly no credit to the company. As a status symbol, it reflected the ultimate in depressed business.

There was no bell, no knocker, and when he rapped on the door with his knuckles he obtained no response. When he tried the door handle the door opened reluctantly and he stepped into a stairwell created by partitioning off the main area of the warehouse leaving only enough space for an old and worn wooden staircase. Simon went up the stairs to the office and inside found the girl, Jean Alcott.

She looked up, saw a fairly good-looking and presentable man, and showed immediate interest. 'Yes?' she asked brightly.

'Could I see the manager, please?'

'Manageress,' Jean corrected, maintaining the smile on her face but withdrawing her eyes from collaboration.

He shrugged. 'Okay,' he conceded, 'manageress.'

'I'm afraid she's had to go out. I expect she's gone to do her shopping, though she *said* it was on business.'

Simon wasn't interested in back-biting. 'When will Miss — ' he began.

'Mrs,' Jean corrected tartly. 'Mrs Marion Shelley. She'll be back when she condescends to return! Now,' her eyes rejoined the business of smiling, 'if I can help — '

Simon had to take a firm grip on himself before instinct had him running from the building. The last person he wanted to get mixed up with was Marion; he had to get away quickly and leave no clue behind.

'I'm Toby Jason,' he said. 'I'm from Mountain Ranch Furs and I — ' He got no further.

'Furs?' Jean cut in, frowning. 'I'm sorry, but I don't see what interest they would be to this firm.'

'Beavers — Furs — Beaver-lamb?' he prompted.

She shook her head and gave a chuckle of genuine amusement. 'I'm sorry,' she said, 'you're on the wrong track. We're into furniture. We wholesale two special brands — Beesuite and Alderplan — but no furs — sorry!'

'I have the oddest feeling my leg's been pulled,' Simon growled ruefully.

The girl's smile became one of reassurance. 'Not by me,' she asserted.

He shook his head. 'No. Some reputed friends — reps staying at my hotel.'

'Oh, dirty trick,' she sympathized.

Simon gestured helplessly and turned towards the door just as it opened and a man in his late fifties entered and stepped aside to let him out. The newcomer wore a clean but well-used lounge-suit and he was vaguely familiar.

'Good morning, Mr Rhodes,' the girl opened — defensively, Simon believed. 'Mrs Shelley is out just now.'

Simon closed the door and hurried down the stairs. He opened the door into the lane and tossed quick glances to left and right to ensure that Marion was nowhere about, then he ran — a schoolboy afraid of being caught scrumping apples.

★    ★    ★

Marion Shelley turned into the lane and stopped short as she saw her former husband hurry away from Beaver's doorway. Instinctively she stepped back into the shelter of the corner and waited for Simon to clear the far end of the alley.

As he rounded the far corner, Marion stepped into the lane once more and hastened across to Beavers'.

On the stairs she came face to face with Henry Rhodes and his expression bore signs of barcly controlled anger.

'Henry,' she stage-whispered lest her voice carried up to Jean Alcott. 'You saw him?'

'Saw who?' he countered shortly.

'Simon!'

'Simon?' He frowned while his mind reorientated. 'Your husband?'

'He was here — just a minute ago.'

'The man who left as I came in, d'you mean?'

'Yes, yes. That was Simon, Simon Shelley.'

Rhodes' face became the epitome of raw anger for just a moment, then calmed and became set in a businesslike expression. 'We'll go up to your office,' he decided. 'Talk business, be natural and for heaven's sake remove that harassed look from your face!'

'But suppose he's been asking questions? Suppose he's been talking?' Marion's agitation raced towards bursting-point.

'We will suppose nothing!' Henry insisted harshly. 'We shall go upstairs in all innocence and in the natural course of things we shall learn all there is to be learned!'

'I have so much to lose,' Marion hissed hysterically.

'And I have more!' he retorted unsympathetically. 'Let us go up.'

Jean Alcott looked up from her typewriter as they entered the outer office. She saw Marion Shelley's flushed face and set smile and assumed that Rhodes' abrupt manner had set her feeling guilty at having slipped out just when their supposedly most valued client had come to do business. Rhodes himself, she noticed, was only slightly more irritable-looking than usual.

Jean would have set little store by their appearance, even so, had it not been for the obvious nervousness with which Mrs Shelley plucked at the fingers of her snug-fitting gloves as though she would pick the leather to pieces if she did not slip them off very soon. And then there was the question:

'Has anyone called while I was out?' Marion's voice trembled as she spoke and there was a nervousness about the way her gaze switched from side to side.

'Before Mr Rhodes,' said Jean dispassionately, 'there was a Mr Toby Jason of Mountain Ranch Furs.'

'Was he here long?' Marion asked.

The girl shrugged, wondering why Marion hadn't asked the man's business. 'A minute or so,' she explained. 'Were you expecting him? I told him furs were not our line and he accepted that a friend had hoaxed him into calling here.'

'You gave him my name?'

'Yes.'

Marion strove desperately to try to stop the trembling in her hands and voice. With a great effort to be calm and businesslike, she said to Henry Rhodes: 'Perhaps we should go into my office.'

If Marion had sought to allay any suspicions in the girl's mind, she failed notably. Jean was fast becoming convinced that there had been more to Toby Jason's visit than met the eye, and while Marion and Rhodes went through to the inner office Jean turned her attention to the built-in stationery cupboard, a fitting with more uses than the obvious. With her head inside it, she could hear virtually every word spoken in the other room.

Henry pushed the door shut and Marion rushed into his arms. 'Oh, Henry, what are we to do?'

'Do? Do? Why should we do anything simply because Toby Jason and your ex-husband are one and the same?'

'He knows I work here and he's seen you here. He can now associate us with each other!'

'What if he does?' Henry scoffed

122

encouragingly. 'What can he do? I sell furniture, you manage a business whole-saling furniture. I see no cause for concern.'

'But the decree,' she said agitatedly. 'The decree absolute! He need only hint at an association other than business and he could turn over the whole thing.'

'You mean that he might suggest you are not as innocent as was claimed in court? We know you are, so what can he hope to prove?'

'He could blackmail *me*,' Marion wailed.

'For money?' Henry snorted derisively.

'For Sarah. For custody of Sarah. He could do that. He's capable of doing it just to spite me!'

Henry held her tightly against him as much to obtain her silence as to encourage her. He wanted to think about the man who had left the office as he arrived. Now he knew it was Simon Shelley, but at that moment he had merely been a vaguely familiar figure. The familiarity had bugged Henry, but at last he had pegged his man. Simon Shelley had been the man in the corridor outside the flat of Mira Feaney, and the realization gave Henry fresh hope — albeit a hope tempered by the knowledge that Shelley could as easily place him at Mira's. For the moment, though, the vital thing was to calm and reassure Marion.

'Shelley may try to pressure you,' he conceded, 'but he can soon be silenced.'

'But how?'

'He has an Achilles heel. If he is disposed to try to take Sarah from you it can only be on grounds of your unsuitability as a mother, and we can counter that very simply by hoisting him with his own petard. There's much more evidence against him this time.'

'Just going with a woman would not be enough,' Marion declared.

'Not just 'a woman',' Henry replied, 'a known prostitute.'

'That Fuhrmann woman again?' Marion pressed.

Henry shook his head. 'No. In any case, that was just a passing thing. This fresh evidence covers several days and a different woman. Frankly, I can't see Mr

Shelley causing any more problems than a yapping dog.'

Marion gazed into his eyes in search of further confirmation. 'How can you know all this?'

'As a precaution I've had Shelley watched.'

'You did this without provocation from him?'

'Provocation?' Henry was puzzled by the observation. 'That's an odd use for the word. Yes, I suppose it could be said I acted without provocation such as we now have, but at least my precaution has proved its worth.'

'Yes, yes.' Marion's words agreed, but her attitude was one of uncertainty. 'And you *will* help me to keep Sarah?'

'Of course, my dear. Whatever I have done in this matter — whatever I have to do — it is all aimed at your ultimate happiness.'

It was some time before Henry managed to calm her and turn her attention to the business which had brought him to the office. That finally completed, he kissed Marion and led the way to the door.

Together they emerged from the inner office and, largely for the benefit of Jean Alcott, they stood for a moment rounding-off their business discussion. It was a waste of effort for she was totally unimpressed by the show. Jean smiled thinly and, so Marion thought, sneeringly as she pinned the pair with her eyes. So effective was she that for a moment they stood as a pair of rabbits held in thrall by a snake.

'Mrs Shelley,' Jean said bluntly, 'I want a pay rise!'

'You — you what?'

'I want a pay rise,' Jean repeated as though speaking to a particularly dense child.

The request was common enough and reasonable enough in the right circumstances but not a subject to be broached so bluntly or openly before a supposed customer. Henry's eyes narrowed, his lips compressed and he frowned heavily but he had the good sense to leave the matter to Marion.

'On what grounds, may I ask?' Marion

demanded, struggling to keep her apprehensions concealed behind a façade of righteous indignation.

'Inflation, cost of living — things like that,' Jean replied offhandedly.

'Which, of course, affect us all,' Marion countered, taking courage from Henry's presence.

'But I do have the burden of hitherto unrealized responsibilities,' the girl added, nodding first at Rhodes and then at the inner office.

Marion's heart plummeted into the depths. 'That man, Jason,' she accused. 'He put you up to this!'

'To what?' Jean was all innocence.

'To this demand,' Marion retorted angrily. 'To this blackmail — for that's what it amounts to.'

Rhodes was reluctant to involve himself too closely at that stage, but he laid a restraining hand upon Marion's arm.

'Blackmail,' Jean suggested with soft menace, 'is a dirty word and your unwarranted accusation constitutes a libel — a gross libel!'

Rhodes felt firmer ground beneath his

feet. 'Libel,' he pointed out firmly, 'refers to the written word. You have nothing from Mrs Shelley in writing. Slander — which is probably what you mean — would require you to produce a witness or two and I'm afraid that as the only witness present I could not, in all honesty, support your claim. There has been no slander.'

'My request was open and straight-forward,' Jean replied, her calm an icy thing. 'It was a demand for Mrs Shelley to pay me my worth in an atmosphere of inflation.'

'Mrs Shelley's hands are tied,' Henry returned sharply. 'She is the manageress here, not the owner.'

'Then untie her hands,' said Jean, quite unimpressed.

'I?'

'Yes,' she snapped, 'you! I am an efficient employee, Mr Rhodes, and I am too experienced not to know that *you* are the boss. Mrs Shelley is indeed manager-ess but she also holds a block of shares, the rest being held by a Mr Rousker and a company called Beverington (Holdings)

Limited. You, Mr Rhodes, *are* Beverington (Holdings) Limited. You hold the bulk of the shares and you are the real boss. Now, untie her hands and allow us to discuss my wage increase!'

Henry's eyes narrowed to slits and his gaze bored into the presumptuous clerk. 'What figure had you in mind?' he demanded.

'Another twenty pounds a week,' said Jean confidently. 'And before you try to tell me you can't afford it, remember that I see the books and I know that you can!'

'It will require some time,' Henry began.

'You can take the decision now,' Jean asserted.

Rhodes nodded. 'That could be true,' he barked, 'but we won't take *any* decision at this moment. You must await *our* decision which will be given in *our* good time. Come, Mrs Shelley, see me out — this matter is closed for the time being.'

'Any delay,' Jean Alcott warned, 'and it's twenty pounds, tax paid!'

'Eight per cent is the best you could

hope for,' Henry countered, 'and not even that if I hear any more of your thinly disguised threats.'

Marion preceded Rhodes down the crude staircase, through the lower doorway and out into the lane.

'Oh, Henry!' She was dangerously close to tears. 'What are we to do?'

'Nothing!' he snorted.

'Nothing? But she will — '

'Alcott will do nothing. When you get back upstairs, tell the little bitch that you'll overlook her audacity for the moment but that she must watch her Ps and Qs in the future. Be firm and add nothing to that. Do not be drawn in any way. She knows her strength can be gauged only by our weakness — our fear of discovery if you will — and if we show quiet resolution as well as indifference to her veiled threats it will be she who is seen to be weak. But be careful, she may not immediately accept the weakness of her position and may attempt to apply stronger pressure. Do not move from your position.'

'Henry, you're sure it will be all right?'

'Trust me,' he insisted.

'I do, I do! But, she — '

'Alcott,' Henry averred harshly, 'will be out of a job before the week is out. A woman of her calibre has, you may wager on it, been at the books. She is altogether too smart and palpably dishonest — it's a near-certainty that she's been lining her pockets at Beaver's expense. This evening I shall return and spend some time on those books. Rest assured I shall find the chink in her defences and, in due course, we'll have in the police to make a formal charge. Let her then speak, let her then accuse us of anything and the world and his wife will cry 'Sour grapes'!'

★　★　★

Simon Shelley cleared the end of the lane and doubled back to his right where he entered the service road on the far side of Beaver's premises from the entrance and office. There were several doorways and gateways in a wide variety of style and occupation but not one led to Beaver's. He covered the road from end-to-end but could find no clue except the one warehouse which should connect with Beaver's office at the far side.

Looking about at the property backing onto the side of the service road opposite the warehouses, he noted that they were old terraced houses long since converted to shops with flats or maisonettes over. The back gates of the shop right opposite 'Carroll and Rogers — Hardware Wholesalers' carried a crude sign stating that it was a greengrocery and florists. He circled the terrace and entered the shop.

It was a small man-and-wife concern, and the female half was a veritable mine of information — mostly gossip, some of it spicy in its own right, some spiced up to make better listening. She had been rounding-off an item relating to 'that sex-mad Biddy Roberts and her no-good long-haired boyfriend' when Simon reached the counter, and she readily answered his questions.

She entered on a long discourse, much embroidered and cluttered with guess-work and asides, and Simon was obliged to edit the whole exchange or become lost in a maze of irrelevancies.

It boiled down to:

Both Carroll and Rogers died after having allowed much of their wholesale hardware business to run down over the past ten years. In time Andrew Rogers, son of the original Rogers, became sole owner and proprietor. Locally he was generally seen as a lethargic young man who cared nothing about business and sold off everything of Carroll and Rogers about twelve months before and went to live in Amdale where he opened a small book and antiques shop.

The yard and old stabling within the former Carroll and Rogers property had since been let off as garaging or secure parking space for people living in the neighbourhood. The upper floors had been taken by Henry Rhodes, the furnisher, for storage of stock.

'Could I get into that yard?' asked Simon. 'I've a notion about buying it but I'd like to look the place over without stirring up a price rise.'

'You'd have to have a key to the yard gate,' the woman's husband cut in. 'Only

Rhodes' staff and the people who garage or park their cars there have keys or right of access.'

'Leaving the private persons out of it for a moment,' Simon said, 'do any vans other than Rhodes' go in and out, d'you know?'

'Yes. Plain ones, mostly.'

'Nothing to distinguish them?'

'Just the name of the van hire company,' the man replied.

'D'you recall that name?'

'I'm sorry, no. I wasn't really interested. All I can tell you is that at least one of Rhodes' regular 'furniture bumpers' was with each van.'

'I believe the vans came from 'Terry's Van Hire',' the woman said.

The husband nodded. 'Yes,' he agreed, 'that would be it.'

'They're at Amdale and Beverington,' Simon said, carefully leading the couple.

'These vans generally come from the Amdale branch,' the man supplied on cue.

Simon left the shop posing possibilities against probabilities and particularly noting the Amdale connection.

# 7

Elaine Rhodes felt her jaw drop and her spirits slump as she heard the report on Simon Shelley.

'Yes,' her father continued, his voice seeming distant to her inward-looking shocked mind, 'he had a woman in his flat for four or five days and she is known to be a London call-girl.'

'Assuming it is any of your business what Simon does,' Elaine began, her voice strengthening as she challenged her father, 'how can you possibly know all this — even if it is true?'

'I have employed a private detective,' Henry replied sharply and defensively. 'He's Stanley Wilkie.'

'The man hired by Marion Shelley to watch her husband?'

Henry sensed that he had made a mistake by giving Wilkie's name. He tried to side-step the issue. 'Possibly,' he agreed disinterestedly. 'The point is that you must see that Shelley is no good.'

'I see no such thing,' Elaine snorted indignantly. 'At the divorce hearing Mr Shelley contended that Wilkie's evidence was untrue and that he visited the Fuhrmann woman on business.'

'And we all know *her* business,' sneered Henry.

'Do we?'

'She is a known — '

'Prostitute? Has she been charged? Has she been convicted?' Elaine challenged.

'I imagine so.'

'You imagine so?' Elaine cried. 'You imagine? Guilty by decree of Henry Rhodes — unless proved innocent!'

'One would be forgiven for imagining you to be retained to defend these people,' Henry suggested sarcastically.

'And you know I have no brief to defend them,' Elaine retorted, 'but in the interests of fair play and in view of the fact that they're not here to answer for themselves I will speak out. My personal objection is to your raising the subject after we had agreed to drop it.'

'You refer, I assume,' Henry corrected

coldly, 'to our agreeing to your not leaving the house?'

'There was no such agreement,' Elaine declared. 'I simply didn't go and you didn't press the matter. We did, however, agree not to discuss Simon Shelley at home.'

'And I respected that agreement. You were able to keep your illusions about the man. But I would not and will not allow myself to be dissuaded from gathering evidence elsewhere.'

'Do you know Simon Shelley?' she demanded.

Henry threw her a sharp glance. 'Of course.'

'You've known him long?'

'Long enough.'

'Exactly how long is 'long enough'?'

'Long enough to know him and all his filthy ways!' Henry barked angrily.

Elaine smiled. 'Yet you needed to hire a private detective to investigate him? Surely, that's the action of a man unsure of his ground? Isn't it the case that you made your wild assertions to me first and then, when I refused to accept them without question, you belatedly set out to obtain proof of your claims? Truth? You weren't interested in proof, only corroboration of your story.'

She drew breath and continued regretfully: 'All my life you've shown yourself to me as a kind, considerate but firm father and a devoted husband. Outside you are known as a cold, calculating, hard-headed businessman, but you brought none of that home. You are cordially disliked — though grudgingly respected — all over town, whereas here you've known nothing but love and respect. Suddenly — triggered, it seems, by the secret codewords 'Simon Shelley' — you have brought your public self into this house and sullied our home. The phenomenon puzzles me and I intend to discover the cause.'

Henry's eyes blazed like solar flares. 'Leave it be,' he growled deep in his throat. 'You may find yourself opening Pandora's Box!'

Elaine slapped her hands onto her hips. 'And whose troubles will be released if I do?' she demanded.

'More people's than you imagine,' Henry snarled.

★　★　★

Under cover of sipping his coffee, Simon studied the schoolteacher across the table. She was quite attractive and her good looks were the kind that would wear well. Elaine, now that she was at last at ease with him, was proving to be a good conversationalist and quietly amusing.

'Right,' he said, smiling at her. 'I've provided dinner, so I think it's time you told me why you rang.'

Elaine's face clouded momentarily and then cleared as she smiled again and said: 'I have to talk to you.'

'Then talk,' he encouraged, 'I'm listening.'

'Not here.' She seemed nervous and hesitant.

'Then where? Your home?' Simon suggested carefully.

'That's the last place.'

'Then, with due caution, may I suggest my place?' he offered.

Elaine tossed back her head in a silent laugh. 'Why 'due caution'?' she asked.

Simon shrugged. 'When you came before,' he explained, 'it was the first time and strictly business so we met in my office. I suspect that this is not exactly business and my flat is the more comfortable place.'

'You feel I may be a little apprehensive about being in your flat, is that it?'

'Something like that,' he acknowledged.

'Well I'm not,' she declared boldly.

Simon nodded. 'When you're ready, then.'

Elaine finished her coffee, grasped her handbag and smiled. 'Ready,' she announced.

He rose, walked round the table and eased away her chair as she stood up. He helped her into her jacket and despatched her to the ladies' room while he settled the bill.

Elaine elected to walk the short distance to Simon's office, it was just far enough to be good exercise after the meal and not far enough to be tiring. On the way they spoke only of inconsequential matters, never once touching upon anything which could give Simon a clue to her real purpose in wishing to see him.

She was a spinster approaching her thirties and he was close to being eligible. He wondered if desperation had driven her to try to make an extra leap year of it.

They reached the office, passed through and went up to the flat, and Elaine was conscious of a tingle of nervous excitement as she entered the traditional pitfall of unmarried girls.

The living-room stretched across the full width of the building above the shop front. It had two windows, one a bay which had provided light for the original front bedroom, and the other a simple sash window where there had once been a small boxroom or bedroom until the dividing wall had been removed.

Elaine thought it was a nice room though the furnishings were unspectacular as was to be expected of a man suddenly reduced to operating on a shoestring. What most impressed her, however, was its neat, clean and comfortable air.

'Drink?' Simon suggested as he helped her with her coat.

'Please.' Elaine felt she needed something to steady her nerves.

'Sherry? Gin? Whisky?'

'A sherry, please,' said Elaine as she perched herself carefully at one end of the settee.

Simon poured a sherry for her and a whisky for himself, and carried them across to the settee where he gave her the drink before seating himself at the opposite end of the settee. She sipped at the sherry, her whole attitude suggesting that she was unsure of where to begin, Simon relaxed and waited patiently for her to break the growing silence.

At last it came. 'Simon, how well do you know my father?'

'Not at all, really,' he replied. 'Today I saw him for the first time in my life — that is to say, the first time I *knew* who he was — but, of course, I know of him through business affairs.'

Elaine looked full into his face. 'You corrected yourself,' she noted, 'over the 'first time'. Had you met him before?'

'I've never *met* him in the accepted sense,' he replied. 'It just happened that I'd been in an office on business and was about to leave when in he walked. I heard the girl clerk say, 'Good afternoon, Mr Rhodes,' so I knew then who he was and I also realized that I'd seen him before but not known him.'

'You'd seen father previously at that same place?'

'No.'

'Somewhere else, then? Somewhere you both have regular business?'

'Possibly your father may have had regular business there, but it was my first time there, too.'

Elaine's expression was one of growing confusion. 'Why are you so confident that there was only one meeting other than today's?'

'Because, so far as I'm aware, that's all there's been,' returned Simon, suppressing a feeling of irritation that the woman would not come to the point. 'That first encounter was no more than a matter of us both being in the same corridor together, it was not a meeting.' He began to suspect that Elaine could be after some evidence of her father's infidelity with Mira Feaney and there was no way he would help her on that score, no matter what her father may, or may not, be.

'Has your business,' Elaine was continuing, 'ever placed you in a position opposed to my father's interests?'

'Not that I'm aware of, but, as your father's interests are wide and latter-day business is all holding companies and front men, I may have taken an opposing position quite unwittingly.'

Elaine fell silent again while she considered the wisdom of her next question. In the end expediency overrode wisdom as a consideration. 'Can you offer me any explanation as to why my father should hate you so intensely?' she posed quietly.

'Hate?' Simon sat up sharply, his puzzled astonishment self-evident. 'Intense dislike?' He paused, momentarily dumbstruck. 'Dislike, perhaps, or distrust in view of the nature of my business. But hate? How could he hate me without a powerful cause? Surely, I'd have some inkling of that?'

'My father does nothing without reason,' Elaine asserted, 'no matter how unreasonable he may seem to those not privy to his thoughts. There just *has* to be a cause.'

'I know of none,' Simon tried to assure her. He frowned as he concentrated his thoughts on a search for any cause at all. 'Tell me,' he asked thoughtfully, 'how did you learn of this — er — hatred?' He handled the word as though it was a hot coal.

'We were talking casually over dinner,' she explained, 'and I mentioned that I'd offered to help the father of one of my girls. He asked who, and I told him: Simon Shelley, father of Sarah Shelley. Father seemed to explode. He heaped abuse on your head such as you'd never meet outside a Victorian novel. I demanded a reason but he couldn't, or wouldn't, give one — at least, nothing of any real consequence.'

Simon pondered this, then said, 'You

realize that my business is essentially confidential so you'll understand I have to be careful what I say in case I injure my clients.' He paused. 'A firm has retained me to investigate and report on Beaver (Wholesale) Limited before my clients do business with them. I called at Beaver's office this afternoon and asked to see the manager. There was a manageress, I was told — Mrs Marion Shelley.'

'Your wife?'

'My wife. Fortunately for me she was out of the office and, since there was no chance she'd give me the time of day, let alone business information, I decided to clear off before she returned. *That* was the moment your father came in and the girl used his name.'

'You're suggesting this afternoon's encounter caused my father's anger?' Elaine asked doubtingly.

'It's all I can offer. I've since learnt that he *is* 'Beaver' so it's possible he resents my nosing into his affairs.'

Elaine took pause for further thought. 'No,' she decided emphatically, 'not

Beaver. I'll swear to it. I know his companies.'

'Might he be a shareholder?' Simon suggested.

'Anything's possible,' she returned with a helpless shrug, 'but I doubt this connection. Tell me, what do Beaver do?'

'They wholesale furniture, chiefly two brands — Beesuite and Alderplan.'

'Ah! Then he would be buying,' Elaine proclaimed. 'He retails both styles. I wonder — could he resent you if he thought you were checking up on his buying?'

'Possibly.'

'Mind you,' Elaine mused, 'that could only explain his attitude today, it cannot explain his initial outburst.'

'When did he first sound off about me?' Simon pressed.

'Last week. On the evening of the day I came to see you.'

'That would be Thursday,' mused Simon.

'Does that make any sense?'

'None that I can think of.'

Elaine frowned thoughtfully. 'How long

before that was it that you first saw him — in that corridor somewhere?'

Simon sensed the need to tread warily along that line of questioning. 'It would be Tuesday of last week,' he said.

'Father was in London on Monday and Tuesday,' Elaine recalled, 'on a buying trip.'

It took all of Simon's self-control to prevent himself laughing. 'That would probably be it,' he agreed. 'I had to go to London myself on Tuesday. I had an appointment after lunch, and as I reached my destination so your father came out of a doorway across the corridor.'

'He recognized you?'

'At the time, I didn't recognize him so I can't say if he knew me.'

'I believe he must have recognized you,' Elaine decided, 'and, knowing the nature of your business, assumed you were spying on him. That would account for his Thursday outburst, and seeing you today at Beaver's may have hardened his suspicions.'

'It makes some sense,' Simon agreed,

happy that neither Angela nor Mira had so far entered Elaine's reckoning.

Elaine fell silent while she mulled over the conversation and finished her glass of sherry.

'Another?' Simon offered.

She held up her glass. 'I'll be daring,' she said, smiling.

Simon took both glasses to the cabinet for refills, only to stand motionless, thinking, then he jerked into action and poured the drinks.

'What,' he asked with studied casualness as he carried the drinks back across the room, 'd'you think of sex?'

Taken aback, Elaine recovered quickly and returned lightly: 'Steady, boy, I've only had one drink.'

'I meant generally, not immediately and personally.'

'Phew! What a relief! I thought, for a moment, that father was right.'

'About what?'

'About this place being a den of iniquity and young women losing their honour here!' A slight flush suffused her face.

'Did he say that?'

'Yes,' she affirmed, 'I'm afraid he did.'

'And what do you think?' Simon asked interestedly.

'I don't know,' she admitted with a mischievous smile. 'I've only been here a short while and already you've plied me with liquor and brought the subject round to sex.'

Simon burst out laughing. 'Purely academically, I assure you. There's nothing personal in it.'

'You mean I'm not your type?'

'What is 'my type'?' Simon posed rhetorically. 'You're an attractive woman and I'm only just coming to know you.'

'But you've had girls up here before.'

'You state that as fact,' Simon observed. 'Why?'

'It was given to me as fact.'

'Suppose it is true,' he replied. 'Does it bother you?'

'Not directly. At least, it shouldn't. You are, after all, a free agent.' Elaine reddened with embarrassment and fell silent.

Simon smiled, believing he understood

her dilemma. 'Your father presented you with this fact?'

'Yes.'

'Today.'

'Yes.'

'Exactly what did your father accuse me of?' he pressed.

'I don't really want to repeat it just now,' Elaine hedged.

'Oh, come off it,' Simon scoffed lightly. 'You came here to unravel a minor mystery and to seek some assurance that I'm not a sex-fiend. Don't back away now!'

'During the past week,' Elaine said in a brief preamble, 'you've had a girl staying here.'

'That's true enough. Her name was Angela Whitney. She had a few days off from her work in London and she came down quite unexpectedly. I put her up.'

'Did you — ' Elaine found it next to impossible to ask directly if Simon had made love to the girl. She felt she was intruding and wasn't even sure she wanted to know, anyway.

Simon took a short cut across the truth

in a determined effort to hold Elaine on the track of her father by diverting her from himself. 'In any twenty-six day cycle,' he reminded her, 'there are times when a woman cannot show too much interest in a sexual relationship. No matter how I felt about it there was no likelihood we could make physical love during that time.'

'You're forthright,' Elaine observed, more than a little embarrassed.

'I feel it was the moment to be,' he returned.

'You knew her condition,' said Elaine thoughtfully. 'How?'

'I've been married for more years than I care to recall,' Simon explained, 'and I can identify the symptoms.'

Elaine found this claim difficult to accept. 'Very well, then,' she challenged. 'How about me — now!'

'Not this week,' he hazarded, 'and probably not next. 'You're a little tense, admittedly, but that's explained by the time, place and conversation.'

He was absolutely correct, and Elaine felt as though she had been stripped and her most personal secrets exposed to the spotlight of public gaze. She sat quietly sipping at her sherry and adopting a contemplative attitude, but the truth was that she was confused and embarrassed.

'Well?' Simon pressed, refusing to let her off the hook, and anxious to know if his ploy had been successful.

Elaine nodded. 'Correct,' she agreed reluctantly.

'Did your father state how long Angela was here?' Simon asked, apparently on the same general theme but bringing Henry Rhodes back into the picture.

'I think he said 'a few days',' she replied with a show of indifference.

'He kept score?'

'He employed a detective named Wilkie.'

'Wilkie is the man who gave evidence of my visit to Rachel Fuhrmann and that evidence was the key factor in Marion's case against me.'

Elaine shrugged. 'I was already aware of that.'

'Do you find it more than a coincidence?' Simon pressed.

'Not entirely. Wilkie, as a private detective working in this locality, is obviously for hire, and if my father felt need of a detective, why not Wilkie? There's probably very little choice in this town.'

'There are three agencies, employing a total of six regulars and the odd part-timer or two,' Simon supplied. 'Wilkie is not local, he was imported and, in fact, this is the second time to my certain knowledge.'

'Just supposing my father did bring in Wilkie from outside,' said Elaine, bridling defensively, 'why would he do so?'

'I was investigating the distribution of shares in a certain company and I was eventually drawn to Rachel. Someone in that company didn't like me prying and they brought in a man unknown to me. He watched me, saw me at Rachel's, and with her reputation it was simple enough to spark off my domestic problems. My error was in allowing the private furore to interfere with the business side and I let the investigation go to pot.

'Now,' he continued, 'it's established

that your father knows Marion and he knows Stan Wilkie. He also has his fingers in more business pies than I could name.'

'You're just guessing much of that.'

'I am, but the hard evidence is too strong to ignore.'

'Accepting purely for argument's sake,' said Elaine slowly, 'that your guess is correct, why would Father bother to tell *me* he had evidence to your detriment? Surely, that could gain him nothing. If you're not investigating the same share structure what would he gain by trying to put you on the defensive?'

'There is the old military maxim that one should pursue the defeated enemy,' Simon replied. 'He may be doing just that.'

'But what can he possibly hope to gain from disclosing these facts to me?' she demanded. 'That can't influence *you*.'

Simon was on the point of considering that Rhodes may have found himself pushed up into some sort of a corner and, like a trapped rat, was conducting an aggressive defence regardless of who got hurt. Suddenly his attention was drawn back to Elaine who was sitting quite still and silent while tears flowed. Uncontrolled and uncontrollable, down her cheeks. Instantly sympathetic and understanding, he held out his arms towards her, inviting her to be comforted. She turned and almost flung herself across the settee to bury her face in his shoulder while she sobbed.

He enclosed her with his arms, providing the haven she so desperately needed, and his right hand caressed her hair consolingly. Words were pointless, and he allowed his hands to say all that was needed — and they were expressive hands.

After a while the sobs eased and the tears abated, but Elaine didn't move from her place of safety for some minutes more, and when she did it was to look up into his eyes with an expression of mixed gratitude and expectancy. Simon kissed her, and she flung an arm about his neck the better to keep their lips pressed together as she returned the kiss with a growing hunger.

'Touch me, Simon,' she pleaded without removing her mouth from his. 'Touch me, please.'

He moved his right hand to fondle her left breast with tenderness and consideration, but her blouse and bra prevented direct contact and he was reluctant to go further until he could be sure of her. Too forceful, and Henry Rhodes' accusations could be given credence in her mind.

Elaine, mostly conscious of her mounting desire, was also conscious of his dilemma, and there was only one way she could urge him on. She unfastened her blouse and freed the fastener of her bra before guiding his hand to her breast again.

Simon caressed her breast, found the flesh firm despite the apparent fullness. He had suspected that she used her bra to hold her breasts high, but now he discovered that it was natural. She made a little sound of approval for what he was doing and returned to the kissing while her desire for him rose towards a demand.

'You have wonderful hands,' she

breathed, and that wonder was expressed in her tone so that he knew her feelings and her needs.

Her body was stirring with sensations she had only dreamt of, and Elaine found herself yearning to rush forward to wider experience. She drew Simon's head to her breasts, and his lips kissed and played over them until she tingled from head to toe and she moved his hand just once more.

Simon felt the growing awareness in her change through a growing desire to a desperate need.

Suddenly Elaine had broken away from him and was getting to her feet and tugging at his hand. 'Now, Simon,' she breathed. 'It has to be now!'

He took her through to the bedroom and they climbed naked into the bed, lips meeting, bodies touching as Elaine experienced that first thrill of total bodily contact.

And then they were making love. He was gentle with her, taking care to guide her along to the moment of fulfilment when a whole galaxy of ecstatic sensations stormed through her body and soul. It was only afterwards, as she lay cradled in Simon's arms regaining her composure, that she was able to enjoy a mental replay and savour each delightful detail. Her tears were long forgotten, only the joy of their union remained, and she smiled in the darkness.

Elaine knew, then, what had been missing from her life — not merely the act of sexual union but the giving and receiving of a very special comfort which only the act of love could bring to its full potential. But she was being academic, she realized suddenly, and smiled guiltily for this was truly the moment to savour the union, not to analyse it.

She drew Simon's head down so that she could kiss him once more; she yearned to let him know how grateful she was that he had at last brought her to womanhood. He caressed her tenderly as he first responded and then took the initiative as they warmed to the exchange. Elaine rejoiced in the tingle of her body under his touch and the new-found power of producing a reaction in him, and she vowed that she would make love with him again — and again — and again if he wanted her. She never wanted to leave his bed.

Suddenly she sat up and switched on the light.

'Something wrong?' Simon asked urgently.

'I've forgotten that Mother's alone in the house,' she explained quickly. 'She's not very well and we've agreed not to leave her alone for any length of time.'

She leant across Simon to study his alarm clock, and as her breasts brushed across him she felt her own desires reawakening and his body reacting to her stimulation.

'It's late,' she whispered hoarsely. 'I should be going — but — '

'Stay.'

'Oh, my God, Simon, I don't want to go. It's been so wonderful here. I never dreamt anything could be so wonderful — but Mother shouldn't be left. Truly she shouldn't. But I want to come again — if you'll have me.'

Simon kissed her lips and her breasts.

'Whenever you feel you need me,' he replied but made no further attempt to dissuade her from her filial duty.

Elaine first knelt up on the bed and then stepped off onto the carpet, her fingers lingering on Simon's naked body as she moved away. He looked at her, nude and shapely, her body beckoning to him and her eyes full of longing for him, but her loyalty drawing her away.

Reluctantly she began to dress, delaying the process of covering her body for as long as she could so that she could enjoy the last lingering caress of his admiring eyes.

'I always knew — ' she said softly — '*knew* mark you, that at this moment, if I ever came to it, I would feel guilty and disgusted with myself, and that I would be too embarrassed to let you look at me.'

Simon began rising from the bed, and he smiled whimsically as he led, 'And now?'

Elaine moved close into his arms, her magnificent breasts meeting his flesh and relishing the renewed contact. 'And now the moment's here I feel neither guilt nor

161

disgust and I want your eyes on me the whole time. I'm not a vain person, but the admiration I see in your eyes makes me feel that I am a desirable woman.'

He kissed her playfully. 'You're that all right,' he affirmed, 'never doubt.'

★　★　★

Henry Rhodes let himself into Beaver's, closing the door behind him and locking it securely. He went up the stairs, through the outer office and set down his briefcase on Marion's desk in the inner office. Pleasurably, he caught a faint hint of her perfume and broke into a relaxed smile which faded quickly as he thought guiltily of Clair left at home alone. Hitherto, Elaine and he had always managed to cover each other's absences from home after normal working hours, but on this occasion the blame for the breakdown of the system could be laid squarely at his own door.

It was he who had persisted in pressing the matter of Simon Shelley and, in anger, Elaine had rejected his request that

162

she should remain at home while he went out 'on business'. He had attempted to explain the importance of his task but, without feeling free to tell her of his problems with Jean Alcott and his love for Marion, he had failed to persuade her. It had been left by Elaine that she would return as early as she could but she would concede no more than that.

Shrugging off his regrets at events, he turned his attention to arranging for Jean Alcott to be visited by her comeuppance.

# 8

Simon rolled his car to a halt outside St Peter's Church which was a convenient point at which to let Elaine off. She had no desire to be driven directly to her home, and in her view the church was quite near enough.

'It's been the most wonderful evening of my life, Simon,' she averred softly as she leant across the seats to kiss him goodnight. 'Thank you.'

He kissed her hard just as he knew she wanted of him and she clung to his neck returning the kiss hungrily. Simon's hand moved inside her jacket and blouse and touched one of her breasts; she pressed it against his palm teasingly, knowing full well that she must soon leave him.

'You're a devil,' he whispered.

'Aren't I though,' she chuckled. 'I've learned so many new things this evening that I'm like a child at Christmas, wanting to try out all its presents at once.

I feel deliciously naughty, and it's a wonderful experience. Some people might call me a wanton — well, I'm not yet, but with you I could soon become one, *and* enjoy it.'

Elaine paused and ran a finger along Simon's lips. 'Was I *very* green?'

He chuckled. 'If you're not the fastest learner,' he replied, 'you're a darned good second. Seriously, though, I don't know what you want to hear from me, but I'll tell you this — once your inhibitions were behind you, you were a tremendous bedmate.'

'Will it always be like that?' she asked.

'Sometimes,' he agreed. 'If the man, the moment, and you are right.'

'And Marion didn't like making love?'

'No.'

'She must have been mad.'

Simon shrugged. 'The man and the moment were never right,' he hazarded.

Elaine's lips brushed his lightly, and she returned: 'I find that hard to believe.'

'Recriminations,' Simon observed pointedly, 'are pointless. It didn't work for us and that's the truth — blame is a tricky thing to apportion.'

'Well, I have my own opinion,' she declared and kissed him again before breaking away and unlatching the door. She was smiling happily when the courtesy light came on and Simon was able to see her face.

'Elaine — ' he began.

She paused in the act of closing the door. 'Yes?'

'Take care not to confuse sex with love. They go better together but neither makes the other come out right.'

'I'll be careful,' she promised, closed the door and was gone.

Simon watched her until she turned a corner and was lost to his view. Only then did he restart the car and head for home. He was unsure of his feelings at that time, except in so far as Elaine worried him in her reaction to him and their love-making. For him it had been a physical and intensely satisfying time yet he had not been in love with her, nor had he 'fancied' her in the first place. 'Lust' in its simplest sense could have made him desire to make love to her, but lust hadn't entered into it and desire had come only after the preliminaries. He began to compare the pleasure of bedding Elaine with the joy of love-making with Angela, and there stumbled upon the reason he had been able to make Elaine's initiation the success she had so longed for. Angela had seen his need and had fulfilled it unselfishly so that he had recovered his confidence and sense of proportion, now he had seen and satisfied Elaine's needs in his turn.

It felt good, but it had not been the love she had secretly been looking for. He could not give real love, he wasn't even sure what it was, but he missed Angela — it was something not to be denied or ignored.

Simon drove the car into the old lean-to garage at the rear of the office, let himself into the building and switched on the light.

The place was a shambles, vandalism taken neat and everything wreckable wrecked. Upstairs the flat was a ruin. He had been away for little more than fifteen or twenty minutes so the job had been quick and deliberate. He touched nothing but did take out his handkerchief with a view to leaving no fingerprints when he phoned for the police. It wasn't necessary, for the telephone lead had been wrenched out and the instrument smashed.

He knew that he should have been boiling with anger, but there was no rage left in him. Trouble had dogged him for far too long to warrant any childish outburst and, resignedly, he went out through the damaged front door to walk to the nearby telephone kiosk. The telephone booth nestled among the bushes screening one of the town's less salubrious public conveniences. Simon opened the kiosk door, picked up the handset and reached out to spin the dial.

'Just bung that back on the cradle,' grated a hard South London voice. 'We'll have no Pigs in on this deal!'

'Pigs?' Simon queried in mock innocence as he began to turn slowly.

'Don't move,' the voice directed warningly. 'Pigs, Fuzz, Cops. We don't want them in on this.'

'Police?' Simon replied. 'Why should I

want the police?'

'Don't get funny with me, squire. No one tries to make a call from a public phone unless they have money ready. At least, they do if they want the fire brigade, the bloodwagon or the police. You've got no fire — yet; no casualty — yet; so you must want the boys in blue. Well, we don't need 'em so long as you remember a few points: You just butt out of other people's affairs in this town *and* you give the dolly-birds a wide berth, too, and you'll survive with your knee-caps intact.'

Simon sensed the slight change in the man's voice and turned from the thighs twisting his shoulders hard. The blow intended for his right kidney jarred its way across his back from hip to hip. He kicked out with a slight stamping motion, catching a knee, shin and foot before he dive-rolled from the booth and across the pavement. Somewhere away off along the half-lit street a woman screamed. Closer at hand a man cursed fluently through teeth gritted with pain.

A fresh voice demanded: 'Where is he, for Chrissake, Harry?'

'Behind the bloody car!' grated the first man angrily, and he advanced on Simon, his heavy boots lashing out as Simon, too late to rise, rolled first one way and then another until one of the boots drove the wind out of him.

His hands gripped the boot and ankle and twisted hard. The man hit the ground and Simon rolled over him, grabbing hair and smashing the man's face into the paving slabs again and again. He seized an arm, twisted it and pressed it against the joint and heard something crack.

The car door scraunched open and a second man got out, his first kick catching Simon full in the ribs before he could react. It drove the breath from his lungs and knocked him sideways off his man. He rolled on and under the partial protection of the rear of another car. The boot caught him once more, hurting, and he tried to struggle away only to find himself hampered by the reflective number plate which effectively pinned him to the ground.

The woman screamed again.

'Stupid cow!' snarled the second man.

He seized his companion and, ignoring the yelps of pain, fairly hurled him into the car before driving off with a howl of protest from hard-pressed tyres.

Shoes thudded on roadway and pavement as people arrived too late — be it by accident or design.

'You all right, mate?' a male voice asked anxiously.

'No I'm not!' Simon gasped feelingly. 'Help me get to the phone.'

'Lie still,' someone urged, 'we'll phone for the ambulance.'

'No ambulance yet,' Simon insisted. 'Let me get to the telephone.'

He was assisted to his feet and supported to the telephone booth where he rested his weight against the side while he lifted the handset and dialled 999. In due course the police were on the line.

'Simon Shelley,' he gasped, '21 Badger Street, Beverington. My place has just been burgled and I've been worked over. The thieves have taken off in a dark-coloured Renault 12TS — the number ends: 2724T — get after them NOW. The passenger can be identified by recent fight injuries!' He hung up then, temporarily spent. If the police needed more information, let them now come to him.

As soon as he could regain his breath, Simon drew money from his pocket and then dialled again. The telephone at the other end was lifted and he thrust a fivepenny piece into the coin slot; Elaine's voice repeated the number.

'Elaine, this is Simon,' he opened.

'You sound strained,' she observed wonderingly.

'Don't I just,' he agreed feelingly. 'Now, get hold of your father and bring him over to my place — fast!'

'But — I don't know — ' she faltered. 'Father's still out.'

'Then you find him,' he gasped forcefully, 'and you get him over here!'

'What's wrong, Simon?' Elaine pressed anxiously. 'Whatever is wrong?'

'Bring your father,' he insisted, 'and see for yourself!' He hung up again, his fury against Henry Rhodes knowing no bounds, and thrusting aside his would-be helpers, he staggered off towards his office.

'Well, sir,' mused Detective Constable Vincent, 'ordinarily I'd have said this was a straight case of vandalism, but if those men were waiting for you to show up at the phone-booth it has to be a case of intimidation here and actual bodily harm there. The timing points clearly to a definite plan.'

'It was,' Simon affirmed. 'I've been leaned on!'

'D'you have any idea who might be behind it, sir?' the detective asked next.

'Not specifically,' replied Simon. 'One thing you don't do in this game is collect friends.'

'But you're not the ordinary run of private investigator,' Vincent observed.

'No, but you can take it from me that crumbly businesses or dodgy businessmen find my work intensely embarrassing.'

'Perhaps you'd let me have a list, sir.'

Simon shook his head. 'I'm sorry,' he said. 'This is where you fall out with me. My business is confidential — it has

173

to be; and to remain so I daren't have you questioning people I may depend on.'

'We might get the man behind the attack,' Vincent suggested hopefully.

'And you might not,' Simon countered. 'I called the police to give them a chance to catch the strong-arm men before they could travel very far. But I'll find the instigator.'

'Within the law, sir,' Vincent warned. 'No freelancing.'

'You nail these two heavies and that will serve notice I'm not easily intimidated. In return, if I find the man who's behind them I'll serve him to you on a plate — so long as there's no risk to my business.'

The detective closed his notebook. 'Very well then, Mr Shelley,' he said, 'I've got all I can for the moment so I'll be on my way.' He paused and eyed Simon appraisingly. 'Perhaps you'll let me run you to the hospital? Your ribs are obviously playing hell with you.'

'Once again I'm sorry,' Simon refused. 'I've two friends coming over very soon now, and when I've spoken with them I'll have them take me over to the hospital!'

A uniformed constable leant in at the front door. 'There's a Miss Rhodes here,' he announced. 'She says Mr Shelley asked her to call.'

Vincent glanced at Simon for confirmation and received his nod.

'Okay,' Vincent agreed, 'let her in.'

Elaine entered the office, a frown of concern on her brow.

Simon introduced her to Vincent, and Elaine nodded a brief acknowledgement before returning her attention to Simon. 'Are you all right?' she asked anxiously. 'Whatever has happened here?'

'Two men roughed me up to warn me off a case,' Simon explained pointedly. 'Someone seems to be finding me an embarrassment.' He waved a hand at the debris about him. 'The damage is not too serious and nothing appears to have been stolen.'

'But you look — ' Elaine began.

'They tried to kick in a few of his ribs,' Vincent cut in quickly. 'He should be in hospital but he insisted on waiting for two people. I assume you are one and I'd suggest you get him to the casualty department as soon as possible.'

'I am the second person, officer.'

Three pairs of eyes turned towards the door where Henry Rhodes stood with the uniformed constable.

'Please come in, Mr Rhodes,' Vincent invited.

'You know me,' Henry observed, his tone brittle.

'Of course, sir,' Vincent replied, his mind busy with conjecture. 'Though I was unaware that you had a daughter.'

'Does that fact have any relevance?' Henry snapped.

'Possibly not, sir,' Vincent admitted offhandedly, 'but I must ask if your visit here is connected with this incident?'

'I think — ' Henry began.

'Not!' Simon finished for him emphatically. 'I asked Miss Rhodes and her father to call on a confidential matter. Now, could we get on with our business?'

'I'm just off, sir,' Vincent replied amenably enough, though his eyes told Simon that he was far from done.

As the door closed behind the policeman, Simon got in the first thrust.

'This job,' he said with a gesture at the wrecked office, 'was accompanied by a warning to me to keep out of the affairs of other people in this town *and* to keep away from the 'dollies' if I don't want to be 'kneecapped'.'

Elaine turned to stare at her father. '*You* arranged this?'

Rhodes frowned angrily at the mess all about him. 'Not I,' he averred fiercely.

'Wilkie,' Simon said with a grunt of pain. It was a shot loosed off into darkness.

★   ★   ★

Henry Rhodes drove Simon's car with the meticulous care he applied to almost everything he undertook. He said: 'You know about Wilkie.'

'Of course, and you've had him tailing me.'

'That's correct,' Rhodes agreed. 'I have strong objections to your association with my daughter — I make no secret of that, and if she hadn't returned home to be near her mother Elaine would confirm it. I found she would not listen to my warnings and so I sought evidence to support my assertions that you are unsuitable company for her.'

'I won't bother to argue the case with you,' replied Simon. 'Nothing I could say would shake you from your castle of bigotry. What I will do, though, is ask why you employed Wilkie?'

'A local man would not have been the wisest to use and, besides, Wilkie had already turned up evidence against you.'

'Wilkie wasn't after me at first,' said Simon, 'he just happened to be on a case leading to Rachel Fuhrmann and our paths crossed. When he reported back to his principal he was told to work me out of my investigation by putting me on the defensive. He could prove I was at Rachel's and a little perjured gilding did the rest. Of course, he succeeded then because my marriage was rocky and I would drop everything to try to keep it from breaking up, but this time I've nothing to lose so I'll fight him *and* the man behind him!'

'You believe Wilkie assaulted you?'

'That would be too obvious,' Simon snorted. 'This was London muscle, some he could import readily enough to do his bidding while keeping him and his principal well out of the picture.'

'Obviously, you believe I am that 'principal',' Rhodes sneered.

'You're employing him.'

'I have given no instructions which could possibly be interpreted as a licence to use violence. I abhor violence.'

'Just what *did* you instruct him to do?' Simon challenged.

'I told him I wanted evidence against you — anything to show you in your true light to Elaine. I told him I was determined that the association must terminate.'

'That's what did it,' Simon averred.

'What is?' asked Henry, confused.

'The last sentence. To a man like Wilkie that sentence was the personification of the old saw: 'A nod's as good as a wink to a blind horse!''

'You honestly believe that?' Henry

demanded in astonishment.

'Too true I do!'

'Frankly,' Henry grated angrily as he recovered himself, 'I find it impossible to accept your theory.'

'Then how else do you see it? You used Wilkie at the time he saw me call on Rachel Fuhrmann and you instructed him to pass the information to my wife — ' Simon got no further.

'I did no such thing,' snapped Henry. 'Wilkie was completely unknown to me before your divorce proceedings. Believe that or not as you will!'

Simon pondered the declaration. Whatever else Henry Rhodes might be, he wasn't renowned as a liar, so it seemed there must be another enemy, one ready willing and able to use Rhodes as an unsuspecting front man. And yet Henry was still an enemy — an implacable but open one.

'You concern yourself with Elaine and me,' Simon said. 'Doesn't it occur to you that at twenty-seven she is old enough to take care of herself and to make her own decisions?'

'Elaine,' Rhodes countered, 'is still a young girl in many ways. In effect she has never left school since she entered it at the age of five. She teaches now, of course, but the environment is the same and the realities of life are virtually unknown to her. A moment's infatuation with a glib philanderer and she could easily make a tragic error marking her for life.'

'And you cast me in this villain's rôle?' Simon growled.

'What else am I to do?' Henry reasoned. 'You offered little more than a token defence against your wife's accusations.'

'All right,' Simon sighed, 'I concede that there's no way for me to convince you any more than I was able to influence the court. Now, tell me this — detesting me as you obviously do, why are you helping me?'

'I concede no guilt in this matter,' Rhodes returned, 'but I do feel that I could have handled Elaine less clumsily and watched my words to Wilkie more closely. In consequence, I am pleased to offer you some small assistance.'

'You're very kind,' Simon acknowledged, and believed that in the glow of street lights he actually saw Henry Rhodes smile. But a wave of bitterness swept over him and he added: 'In return, I shall not mention seeing you at Mira Feaney's last week.'

If there had been a smile there at all, if the brief quirk of the lips had not been a trick of the light, then it was torn away and the brows knit together above eyes suddenly imbued with blazing fires.

'You overreach yourself, Shelley, if you believe — '

'I express no belief. I merely point up the old adage about glass houses and stones.'

The conversation ended as they reached the hospital's casualty department. Rhodes helped Simon from the car and kept a watchful eye and hand ready until trained people took over, and then he bore himself with surprising patience while Simon was examined and treated.

At last Simon returned to the waiting area duly certified as suffering nothing more serious than severe bruising and abrasions. Henry tossed aside an aged copy of *Reader's Digest*, rose to meet him and escort him back home.

As they drew up before Simon's office Simon thanked him again for his time and assistance, but Henry brushed it all aside and saw him safely inside before garaging the car and heading for his own home.

★　★　★

It was one-thirty in the morning when Elaine heard her father's car enter the short driveway of their home. She waited for him to enter the house, and then she appeared at the lounge doorway to ask bluntly: 'Coffee?'

'Yes please,' Henry returned, although he really wished for nothing more than to get off to his bed. His intuition told him that his daughter had waited up solely to initiate an 'air-clearing' operation, and he was willing to concede that it was a necessary thing. He followed her through to the kitchen: 'How's your mother?' he asked.

'Sound asleep and perfectly all right,' replied Elaine curtly, 'and before any pointless recriminations are hurled about, I believe we should agree that any guilt about leaving her alone is distributed equally between us!'

'Agreed,' Henry sighed.

'I trust,' Elaine continued, her words coming staccato and harsh in her still unaccustomed rôle of a woman in her own right, 'that you are satisfied with the outcome of your interference in what was really none of your business?'

'We don't know with any certainty that the attack on Shelley is the result of anything instigated by me,' Henry countered defensively.

'Suppose it comes out that Wilkie did, in fact, arrange the attack on Simon,' Elaine posed, 'what will you do? Tell the police?'

'Such an action would be the height of stupidity,' Henry snorted.

'And what is so stupid about honesty?' Elaine demanded indignantly.

'My original aim was good and honest,'

Henry returned, 'and the fact that something unexpected has occurred has no bearing upon that. To be swayed by the emotions of the moment would undo the whole purpose of the exercise.'

'Exercise?' Elaine fumed. 'Is that how you see this? An impersonal exercise?'

'It was,' Henry explained quietly, 'an honest effort to prevent you making an utter fool of yourself. Had you not become infatuated with Shelley our paths would not have crossed.'

'You're saving me from my own folly, is that it?' she jeered.

'If you choose to put it that way, yes.'

'Well,' Elaine grated fiercely, her eyes ablaze, 'your efforts are having the reverse effect and driving me into his arms!'

'So you've overstepped good sense,' Henry observed sadly.

'What *is* good sense?' Elaine demanded.

'You will continue to see Shelley despite all this and my objections?'

'I certainly will,' she declared forthrightly, 'no matter what you say or do!'

'Then you must look to your own

affairs,' Henry replied, 'as I must look to mine.'

She eyed him coldly. 'You know, I'm almost coming to suspect that this overreaction to my friendship with Simon has its roots elsewhere.'

'Elsewhere?'

'Business. You were at Beaver's the wholesalers yesterday and the manageress there is Marion Shelley — Simon's ex-wife.'

'What of it?'

'Simon saw you there and he believes you own Beaver's, he also knows of Marion's position. Frankly, I believe your presence there may have tied you to a firm you prefer not to be known to own and you've seen the potential danger.'

'You're convinced I'm behind tonight's attack?' Henry sneered.

'Aren't you?' she retorted.

Henry Rhodes did not look a bold man, but boldness and an unerring talent for seizing the main chance were keys to his modest success. 'You're quite sure,' he sneered, 'that you wouldn't care to go the whole hog and claim that I have a more personal association with Mrs Shelley?'

The stroke paid off. 'Oh, Dad!' Elaine chided. 'Let's not become reduced to childishness. You know very well that I could never accuse you of such a thing, you love Mother far too much.'

# 9

Jean Alcott smiled mockingly as Simon waved her to a chair, one of the two he had managed to salvage for office use.

'You appear somewhat pained to see me,' she suggested. 'Is my presence here so embarrassing?'

Simon pulled a wry grin. 'If you imagine that,' he returned, 'I suggest you go out again and make a fresh entry. For the record, I have quite a number of bruises and abrasions as a result of being worked over last night. As to being embarrassed — you don't really know me, so don't guess. Now, how may I help you.'

'I've come to offer you some information.'

'I deal in information,' Simon acknowledged unhelpfully.

'Do you pay for it?'

'On occasion, though it would depend upon its worth.'

'Twenty-five pounds, cash on the nail,' Jean announced.

'For what?' he asked offhandedly.

'Some information you need.'

Simon pursed his lips and screwed up his nose. 'What information could I possibly need from you?' he wondered.

Jean's face hardened. 'Don't play games with me,' she snapped. 'I'm not in the mood for it and you're in no position to fence. Do I get the money?'

'Only if you can offer something worth the outlay,' Simon returned. 'I'm not a philanthropist.'

'Money on the table or no information,' Jean insisted, her lips setting in a determined line as she finished speaking.

'The door's that way,' said Simon, pointing past her and returning his attention to the papers on his desk.

The girl rose, turned abruptly and stalked towards the door, her whole bearing revealing that she was expecting him to call her back, but Simon wasn't so easily swayed. She had her hand on the door-handle and still he was letting her go. Jean halted, turned and warned:

'You may regret it!'

'My life,' Simon observed wearily, 'is filled with regrets. I'll manage.'

'You're a fool!'

'Possibly,' he conceded willingly.

'Twenty!'

'Twenty what?' Simon asked innocently.

'Pounds.'

'For what?'

'Oh my God! Are you determined to stay on that track?'

Simon looked directly into her eyes. 'Even at five pence,' he affirmed coldly.

The girl returned to her seat. 'You're a hard swine,' she asserted.

'True,' Simon agreed softly. 'And you're desperate. Now, let me hazard a guess. You've been given the boot from Beaver's and you don't like it so you're seeking revenge. You've come here to sell me the information that: (a) Henry Rhodes is having it away with my former wife and (b) that he virtually owns Beaver's through one of his holding companies. You are soon to be charged with embezzlement and you're scratching around trying to raise enough money for your bail.' He smiled deprecatingly. 'I read people's minds, you know.'

'Like I said, you're hard, Shelley!'

'You don't know the half of it yet,' Simon grinned as he picked up the telephone and dialled a number. Jean resisted a temptation to run and waited uncertainly, her eyes darting quickly from side to side like a trapped animal.

'Marion?' said Simon when the connection was made. 'Simon — this is a business matter.'

'Very well then,' Marion agreed reluctantly. 'Go ahead.'

'I have Jean Alcott in the office — '

'I fired her this morning,' Marion cut in. 'It appears she's been at the books.'

'She's offering me information about Beaver's and about you.'

'D'you intend to use it?'

'If I did,' he replied, 'I'd hardly be bothering to tell you, now would I? I just thought it only fair that you and your directors should know she has her knife in your back and is quite capable of twisting it.'

'Thank you,' Marion returned, her gratitude genuine, if tinged with a little embarrassment.

Simon replaced the receiver and smiled at the girl. She opened her mouth to speak, but he raised a restraining hand.

'I know,' he said with a cheeky grin, 'I was born on the wrong side of the blanket!' He began to chuckle but that was nipped in the bud as his battered ribs jabbed at him.

The girl's eyes changed. They narrowed and the rising anger lighting them was suppressed. 'If you won't help me one way,' she said, 'maybe you will another.'

'I doubt that,' returned Simon, 'but tell me anyway.'

'There's work for a clerk here,' Jean declared.

'You're absolutely right,' he agreed. 'I used to have a girl but I had to let her go when business tailed off due to my preoccupation with my divorce. I couldn't afford the wages any more.'

'That's all behind you,' Jean urged. 'I could organize the office side while you had more time to make money.'

Simon shook his head. 'Sorry. I don't like your references.'

'I'm innocent until *proved* guilty,' Jean protested. 'Your wife found nothing wrong with them. Henry Rhodes must have gone over them just looking for excuses to sack me.'

'There's always the industrial tribunal,' Simon suggested. ' 'Wrongful dismissal' should be easy to prove — if you're right! And, of course, you're correct about Marion. In many ways she can be too trusting. Show her some slick bookkeeping and she would be impressed by the skill and neatness rather than suspicious of the agile mind behind it.'

Jean tried another approach. She was becoming desperate — having gone to him to try to make life miserable for Marion Shelley and Henry Rhodes she found herself getting nowhere so she made a final effort. 'Rhodes is having an affair with your wife! Don't you care?'

'Why should I care? If Henry can get anywhere with her, good luck to him.' Simon paused and allowed the bland smile to slip from his face. 'Now,' he said ominously, 'I suggest you get out of here before you get yourself into any more trouble.'

'You're a — '

'Spare my blushes,' Simon begged.

★   ★   ★

'Don't you think Jean Alcott will try to get back at us through the court?' Marion asked apprehensively.

Rhodes shrugged. 'One can't be sure of these things, my dear,' he said thoughtfully. 'Women of her calibre are predictable only up to a certain point — in her case pure vindictiveness may set her tongue working.'

'Can we do nothing to silence her?'

'I believe we can,' Henry replied absently, still with his mind ranging over broader fields. 'I believe it could be arranged for a further charge of attempted blackmail to be put to her, in which case we could be anonymous no matter what she might choose to say.'

'Oh, Henry,' said Marion, pressing close to him, 'I do so hope you're right.'

Henry hugged her tightly in an effort to transmit to her some of his courage, but the truth was that fear is the more contagious and he experienced vague doubts about his intentions and their anticipated outcome. Generally he had been able to make sound judgements, base plans upon them and watch those plans come to fruition, but he had to acknowledge that in the case of Elaine and Shelley he had run into problems and he wondered if Jean Alcott would prove as troublesome.

'And now there's Simon's intrusion to contend with,' Marion murmured.

'Shelley will not bother us,' Henry asserted confidently.

'How can you be so sure?' she asked doubtingly.

'Oddly enough, although I must oppose him strongly, for business and personal reasons I have come to trust him and his word. Can you, in all honesty, cite any important occasion upon which he went back on his word or actually cheated?'

'Don't you count our marriage vows?' Marion demanded. 'He cheated on those when he went with that Fuhrmann woman.'

'I believe it would be unwise to take too much cognisance of that,' Henry cautioned. 'Since I have had some experience of this man Wilkie, I find I am inclined to accept that some, at least, of his evidence may have amounted to perjury.'

Leaning back against his encircling arms, Marion looked up into Henry's face. 'You mean the decree absolute may be held up?'

Henry shook his head. 'No. There will be no hold-up if everyone holds their tongue. You no longer want Simon, do you? And he is not interested in you. It amounts to divorce by consent. But that is by the way; my point is Wilkie — I have strong suspicions about him.'

'Of what do you suspect him?' Marion pressed.

'It's an intuitive thing at the moment,' Henry replied, 'and something I can't readily explain.'

'What I can't understand,' Marion said, 'is how you can now speak so assuredly of Simon when, very recently, you spoke so vehemently against him.'

'Shall we just leave it that Shelley and I have met, talked, and come to an understanding? A somewhat tacit agreement, I admit, and rather fragile at the edges but, none the less, an understanding.'

'Will Simon stop investigating Beaver's now?' Marion asked anxiously.

'Possibly not,' Henry replied, 'he has a job to do — whatever I may think of him nosing around. Frankly, it doesn't concern me, Beaver's is far from being our Achilles heel. So long as he sticks to a business investigation it won't matter a jot.' He drew a long breath. 'And now, my dear,' he continued, 'I must be going. There is much work to be done at my office. I shall have a reliable agency girl sent round to help you until we can advertise for a permanent replacement for the Alcott girl.'

Marion smiled wanly, barely putting a brave face on her fears.

Henry kissed her protectively and then lovingly, only then discovering that such manifestations of his affection for her were becoming a chore. Irritated with himself, he shrugged off his growing disquiet and went about the day's business.

\* \* \*

Detective Constable Vincent entered Simon's office and stood for a moment appraising the victim of the previous night's violence. 'Good afternoon, Mr Shelley,' he opened. 'Is it okay if we talk?'

Simon smiled. 'Of course, sit down.' He waved towards the chair lately vacated by Jean Alcott. 'I've just made some tea,' he invited.

'I'd love a cup,' Vincent sighed as he eased himself onto the chair. 'I'm parched.'

As he poured the tea, Simon asked: 'Have you had any luck with my visitors?'

'I'd like you to come down to the station,' Vincent replied, adding hurriedly, '*After* the cup of tea. We'll be setting up an identification parade.'

'Glad to oblige,' Simon replied, 'but I warned you last night that I saw little or nothing of faces.'

'That's understood, sir, but I think you should have a look at them anyway — even if only as a formality. We do have two other witnesses who did see faces.'

'Fair enough,' agreed Simon. 'I just wouldn't want you to be relying too heavily on me.'

'We won't,' Vincent said, 'but there's one area where you could be of assistance if you were willing.'

'How could I assist you?' Simon asked cautiously.

'Tell me what you've been working on so that I can get after the people behind this attack.'

'No chance,' Simon insisted regretfully. 'I'm genuinely sorry about it but I daren't risk a breach of confidence.'

'Well, I tried,' Vincent consoled himself and took a drink of his tea. 'I thought, maybe, Rhodes is behind it. He's a sharp businessman and he can be vindictive. We've another case involving him.'

'Jean Alcott, embezzlement,' Simon said flatly.

'Rhodes told you?'

'No. She did, indirectly.'

'Your wife's manageress at Beaver's,' Vincent observed.

'Ex-wife,' Simon corrected. 'We're newly divorced.'

'I'm sorry,' Vincent returned lamely.

'Don't be. It's a good thing.'

'Rhodes does plenty of business with that firm.'

Simon grinned broadly. 'You're fishing,' he said.

'There's fish in the pool,' declared Vincent, maintaining the analogy, 'and I've got an echo-sounder.'

'I'll agree that you may have some basis for *suspecting* that Rhodes may have had something to do with me being worked over,' Simon agreed, 'but I'm confident you're wrong. He had nothing to do with it.'

'I wish I could feel as certain,' Vincent replied feelingly. 'Your ex-wife at Beaver's; Rhodes at Beaver's.'

'You're suggesting he's chasing me off?'

'Why not?' Vincent countered.

Simon shook his head and shrugged. 'If Henry Rhodes fancies Marion, that's between the two of them. Frankly, I think he'd be a damned fool if he did — but that's his business. I'm no danger to him there and I'm sure he must know it. I contested the divorce largely in the interests of keeping the family unit together for our daughter's sake, but the judgement has been handed down and at least I'm free of Marion — that counts for a lot!'

Vincent was a relatively young man who, after a long period in the uniformed branch, had been switched to CID where he was quietly building a firm base upon which to construct his future in the county police force. Rarely, if ever, did he play the heavy hand. More often than not he was seemingly slow and deceptively soft but his record showed a persistent habit of achieving results.

'I've spoken to Mr Rhodes,' he said. 'He wasn't very helpful.'

'I don't see how he could be,' Simon returned.

'When I came away from his office,' Vincent continued almost musingly, 'there was a man waiting to see him. I know the man — Stan Wilkie — a private detective who used to work in London but more recently he's been operating from Amdale. He had a reputation in London as a top man at hire purchase 'snatch-backs' and a good connection with an auctioneer on the resale side of repossessed cars.'

'Wilkie seems a nice sort of chap,' Simon observed. 'I gather you've looked him up in the 'Who's Who on the Fringe of Crime'.'

'Just once,' said Vincent significantly, 'he was 'done' for GBH. After that he never became personally involved in the rough stuff.'

'So?'

'So I find myself intrigued by multiple coincidences. Such as Wilkie operating in Beverington more frequently these days; of him giving evidence at your divorce hearing; of him being at Henry Rhodes' office today; of Henry clearly having no love for you; of you being 'leaned on'; and your claim that your attackers spoke with South London accents. All these things fascinate me.' Vincent smiled amiably and turned his attention to finishing off his cup of tea.

Simon returned the smile in equal measure. 'As you said, there are fish in the pool. Your trouble is that you're fishing in the wrong pool as well as using the wrong tackle.'

'You could be right,' Vincent acknowledged readily enough, 'and I'm willing to keep an open mind on the matter, but you'd better believe me that this Wilkie is a right villain and he'll bear watching.'

'Because of the GBH?' Simon doubted. 'A single conviction? One swallow doth not a summer make.'

'That's true, but that little bird comes instinctively in search of its preferred environment.'

Once again Simon could not resist a smile of respect for the man. 'It's your guess, then, that Wilkie finds the environment in this county more amenable than his old London haunts? Doesn't it strike you that he may have been chased out?'

'I think not,' Vincent replied soberly. 'All the evidence suggests that Wilkie is not a man who pushes easily. He has quite a record of defiance of the London gangs and there's good reason to believe he virtually destroyed two gangs trying to extend their 'protection' business into a new area of prostitution.'

'By 'area' do you mean 'locality'?'

'No. I mean a format different from the street-walker/call-girl line of country.'

'He was 'minder' for a new chain of brothels?'

'Not at all. The story — and it is only a story — is that someone had a small-scale private girlie business arrangement going and an enterprising gang looked for a way to grab a chunk of the profits. Wilkie was hired to chase them off, and he did. That wasn't even his regular line of work — just another job, executed and paid for. I'll swear nobody has driven him out of London.'

'So who or what is he after down this way?' Simon posed.

'Why don't you tell *me*,' Vincent suggested with a grin.

★　★　★

Simon drove himself down to the police station and found the trip well worth while when he was able to identify one of his assailants.

Two women who had seen the line-up ahead of him identified two men, one of them the man he picked out. Later he was able to observe the two away from the parade. They were typical hired muscle. Pay them, tell them who needs a hammering and they'll drift off, do the job without malice, go for a pint and discuss the race-cards for the following day's race meetings. No imagination. No knowledge of, or interest in, the whys and wherefores of their act.

Vincent charged them and they were tucked away in the cells.

Up to a point Simon was satisfied with the outcome, but on his way back to the office he was very thoughtful.

Elaine was already at his flat, having let herself in. She welcomed him home with a kiss and fussed about him before settling down to prepare tea.

'You really should get some rest instead

of trying to get back to work so soon,' she chided.

'I've been here all day,' Simon defended, 'except to drive down to the nick just now.'

'Is that policeman getting anywhere?' Elaine asked.

'They've rounded up a couple of small-time muscle men and charged them. I have an idea there was a third man somewhere.'

'You've told the police?'

Simon shook his head. 'No, it's little more than intuition.'

'Have they any idea who may be behind it?'

'None.'

'Have you?'

Simon sighed heavily, the movement of his chest making his ribs ache. He winced and drew a look of concern from Elaine. 'Not exactly,' he admitted. 'There are a whole flock of wild ideas chasing about in my head, and one of them is the right one — but which?'

She let her gaze drop towards the table. 'I feel guilty,' she confessed.

He frowned. 'You? About last evening?'

Elaine smiled fleetingly while she said, 'Oh no! Not that! How could anyone feel guilty about anything so wonderful?'

'Then why?'

It was a little time before she replied, for she needed to consider her feelings on the matter.

'Am I terribly wrong to suspect my father so strongly?' she whispered.

Simon nodded. 'I believe so — not just because he is your father and that you would be expected to respect and trust him. In my view those things — respect and trust — must be earned whether one is a parent or not. No one has an automatic right to them nor an automatic duty to give them. In your father's case, I believe you should respect his motives and trust him to do the right thing from this point on.'

'By that you imply that he *has* been untrustworthy,' she charged.

'No. What I'm suggesting is that your father made a mistake in his handling of Stan Wilkie and, stubborn though he may be, he can now see his error and will not repeat it. Your father is an astute businessman, there's no denying, but he has little or no understanding of Wilkie and his type.'

'You can defend him?' she marvelled. 'Even though he has gone to such lengths in his efforts to keep us apart?'

Simon shrugged. 'I'm a father. I have an only daughter. I can guess his emotions and his protective instincts. He is a man who takes his parental duties seriously but I'm certain he won't interfere again.'

'You can't be so sure,' Elaine doubted sadly.

'But I am, none the less.'

'I wish I were as certain,' she sighed fervently.

'Would it help,' asked Simon, smiling with sympathy and understanding, 'if I tell you that I believe that the major key to what this is really all about lies in London and not down here?'

'Why London?'

'Wilkie is a London man. Rachel Fuhrmann moved here from London. I'm convinced that Wilkie was watching her on behalf of someone — possibly someone with business interests in London — and when he reported that I was making inquiries at her place he was told to deter me without being too obvious about it. Whether he or his principal hit on the idea of striking at my marriage, I don't know, but it worked fine until the decree nisi and last week I went back to have a few words with Rachel.'

'Father has business connections in London,' Elaine reminded him, 'and he's employing Wilkie right now.'

'My guess is that it's pure coincidence,' replied Simon, 'and the fact that Wilkie was working for your father doesn't mean that he had ceased to work for any former client. If, in keeping an eye on me, he saw me return to Rachel's place, he was entitled to assume I was restarting where I left off and to report back to the other client. The current set-up could easily provide a cover for the use of the 'heavies' to warn me off. Wilkie is an opportunist. Wilkie's only real handicap in all this is that he's too new around here, he sticks out like a sore thumb or, to find a better analogy, he's like a pike turned loose in a goldfish pond.'

'Just how dangerous is this Wilkie?' Elaine asked.

'Very dangerous, I should think. By that I don't mean that he is a direct threat, it's more a matter of him reacting to circumstances and causing reactions in others. You know how it is in schools — there's always one child, at least, who always seems to be the one to drop things or make silly mistakes, no matter how they try. I believe Wilkie must be a man quite unable to avoid generating trouble.'

Further conversation was interrupted by a sound downstairs. Elaine went down to investigate and returned with Sarah whose emotions were confused because the presence of a teacher tended to set her on guard though she was very concerned for her father's injuries and secretly delighted to find Miss Rhodes and her father taking tea together.

'How are you, Dad?' Sarah asked, giving him a kiss.

Simon smiled back reassuringly. 'Not too bad really,' he replied, 'just bruised and feeling a little bit stiff.' He eyed her carefully. 'Does your Mum know you're coming here?'

'She told me you'd been mugged or something — someone at work told her — and she said it would be all right if I popped in to see you.'

'Well, it's good of you to come, love,' he replied, 'and it's nice to be able to tell you I'm okay.'

'What happened, then?'

Elaine fetched a third cup and saucer and poured tea for Sarah while the girl listened, amused, to the airy yarn spun by Simon. At the end, Sarah gazed askance at her father.

'Now that was a lovely fairy tale, Dad,' she congratulated, 'but I'd much rather have had the 'X' certificate version. Which did he tell you, Miss Rhodes?'

Elaine smiled broadly, but her eyes retained a serious air. 'I came in at the end of the real-life 'X' version,' she replied, 'and, to me, it looked far from amusing.' To Simon she said: 'Sarah is no longer a little girl, Simon, she is on the threshold of adult life, adult experience

211

and adult understanding.'

'Well said, Miss Rhodes,' Sarah applauded gleefully before falling into a wondering silence as the eyes of her father and teacher met to exchange glances which seemed to carry some deep meaning.

Sarah emptied her tea-cup and later helped Elaine to do the washing-up.

'How long will you be able to stay with your father?' Elaine asked as they stood at the sink.

Sarah hesitated before replying. As much as she wished to be near her father, she had no intention of undoing her own dreams for him by 'playing gooseberry'. 'I had no special time,' she said at last, 'but — '

'Your father may sound quite bright,' Elaine explained, seizing her opportunity, 'but he has suffered a worse beating than he shows. Just now he should rest more than do anything else but unless someone keeps a close eye on him I don't believe he will. I'd stay on myself but I must go home for a while because of my mother's health. My father should be home later and I can return, but in the mean-time — '

'In the meantime,' said Sarah, 'I shall keep him in order.'

'Would you?'

'Of course. I'll just give Mum a ring and say that I'm staying on for a while.' Sarah looked momentarily embarrassed. 'I won't bother to mention you, Miss.'

'That would be best,' Elaine agreed, relieved.

They completed the washing-up together, and then Elaine took her leave, promising to return as soon as possible.

Father and daughter were alone and seated on the settee. They spoke of his injuries and Elaine's presence and then fell silent for a while.

Simon looked about for something to suggest. 'D'you want the television on?' he asked.

'No thanks, Dad,' she returned, 'it's a load of rubbish these days. I'd rather talk.'

He smiled. 'Just when I thought conversation had become a thing of the past,' Simon said. 'Name your subject.'

'You and Miss Rhodes.'

'Ah!'

Sarah took a turn at smiling. 'Ah, what?' she demanded. 'Have you suddenly lost interest in conversation?'

Simon shook his head. 'No. I simply suspect that you may be overreaching.'

'How close are you and Miss Rhodes?'

What could he say to that without torpedoing Elaine's image at the school? 'I kissed her goodnight yesterday evening.'

'Oh, big deal! How do you *feel* about her?'

'I like her. She's a nice person once you get to know her.'

'I *knew* you'd like her,' Sarah enthused. 'Now you must ask her out to dinner.'

'That was last night,' he grinned. 'Give me a new idea.'

'Did it go well?'

'You're very pushy.'

'Did it go well?' she persisted.

'It went well,' Simon conceded.

'And afterwards?'

'I dropped her home and came back here to find the place upside down.'

'Dad,' Sarah asked cautiously, 'what are

you going to do about her?'

Simon smiled whimsically. 'Could you be more specific?'

'Well, d'you really go for her? D'you fancy her? How serious is it with you?'

'Are you really asking about marriage?' he said seriously.

'Yes. If you want it straight,' Sarah returned, 'I'm talking about marriage. You're not really bachelor material, Dad, you need a woman to come home to. Miss Rhodes can be very nice and I know she digs you. You could do a lot worse than marry her.'

'Listen, love,' Simon replied, 'you're right, I'm not a loner by nature and I do need a wife to care for, but it's too soon yet for me to be at all sure of who I want. Miss Rhodes *is* nice and we seem to get on like a house on fire, but it's far too early to think of marriage to anyone, not just her. She's so nice I could marry her for that alone — the difference from your mother's attitude to me — and only later find out I'd married on the rebound. You wouldn't want that for us, would you?'

Sarah frowned. 'Oh no, Dad, that

would be as bad, or worse. I don't really mean to interfere, but Miss Rhodes is alone and you're alone — '

'And you've brought us together,' he ended for her. 'I don't believe you'll find either of us ungrateful for that, but the time has come for you to leave us to find our own way from here. And,' he cautioned, 'you mustn't be upset if, in due course, we find we're not suited for marriage.'

She smiled a little sadly and said, 'Okay, I'll try not to push any more, but I'm sure you're right for each other.'

'For your sake,' he said, 'let's hope you're right, but I'll make no promises at this stage.'

It was about seven-thirty when Elaine returned, and the first thing she did was drive Sarah home. The girl twice found herself on the point of asking Elaine how she felt about Simon, but each time remembered her promise to her father. Even so, she dearly longed to know how the teacher felt, but Elaine did not broach the subject and so Sarah had no opportunity to learn anything.

As Sarah entered the front gate of her home, Elaine turned the car and headed back towards Simon's office, a smile upon her face and her pulse quickening in anticipation of what she hoped was to come. She parked the car and let herself into the office where she paused to smooth her skirt and pat her hair before climbing the stairs to the flat.

Simon waited patiently for her return. He still felt stiff and sore but he was prepared to meet the needs which he suspected had brought Elaine back to him, and he looked forward to her arrival.

She came into the living-room smiling a little shyly as she realized that they both knew very well just what would be the outcome of the evening. At first, despite her longing to be close to Simon, she held herself aloof, frightened of what he would think of her, but before long they had kissed and she was secure again in his arms, the touch of him sending her pulse racing once more as she drew his head down and kissed him with a growing and burning hunger.

His hand moved tenderly over her

breasts, and without further delay she unfastened her blouse and drew it back to reveal that she wore no bra. She had prepared for this moment, hoping it would come and wishing to have his sensitive hands moulding and caressing her breasts again. Her lips parted and she waited eagerly to each new step towards the delight she had experienced barely twenty-four hours previously.

Elaine pressed hard into his hand, moving her body sensuously so that his body responded. Suddenly Simon stood up, scooped her into his arms and took her off to his bedroom. They undressed, each helping the other; pausing to kiss and going on to the point where they were naked in bed, their bodies pressed hard against each other. Simon felt the protests lodged by his bruises and abrasions, but he ignored them in favour of meeting the growing demands of the eager young woman beside him.

At last they were making love; Elaine with a joyous anticipation of the ecstatic moment soon to sweep over her; Simon with the sheer pleasure to be had with a beautiful and eager woman. The moment came, and Elaine felt that she could well die from the sheer force of the wave of sensual fulfilment which crashed through her excited body.

The great wave swept on, leaving Elaine in a calm area, her breathing still a little laboured, her pulse racing on and her mind focused only upon their love-making. If it were possible, this time was even better than before, and she wondered how much better it could be without totally exhausting her. She pressed her lips to Simon's, kissing him fiercely and feeling his response. Their lips parted and began to search each other's faces for fresh places to kiss, and then her hands seized the sides of his head, pressing it down towards her breasts so that his lips could toy with her proud, hard nipples.

It was strange how she felt momentarily spent and yet experienced no abatement in the force of her desire, but she had the sense to realize that she must relax a while before satisfying her desire once more.

Simon moved onto his back and Elaine turned to lay against his flank; her breasts resting on his chest were a constant reminder to him of what had been and what was to be.

They didn't speak — it would have been a pointless exercise anyway — their lips and bodies provided all the exchanges necessary. Elaine felt the burning needs of her body again making themselves known, and she began encouraging Simon once more.

She lifted herself and teased him by brushing the tips of her breasts across his body and face, removing them out of range of his lips at just the moment they reached out to kiss her. And she knew the joy and pride of seeing the admiration in his eyes.

'I'm attractive,' she told herself with some surprise. 'Staid old Elaine Rhodes has a body which can turn on a man almost at will. I can start him off just when I want to and I can keep him going right to the end — the wonderful end.'

# 10

Rachel Fuhrmann was, if such a thing could be possible, even less eager to see Simon than she would have been to open her door to a king cobra.

'Clear off!' she snapped.

Simon had been wise enough to wear his heavy shoes and so he could thrust his 'salesman's foot' inside the door-jamb with relative impunity. 'No,' he said with a cold finality. 'Not this time!'

'You're trespassing!'

He shrugged. 'So sue me! Or, better still, call the police — specifically, call Detective Constable Vincent!'

Rachel frowned and hesitated. She had no direct fear of the police, legally she was completely in the right and could count upon their support, but there was now something very different about Simon — it made her uncertain and that uncertainty led to indecision. Why was he suddenly so cold and hard, so willing for her to call the police? He wanted answers to his questions. The police would want to know why he had called on her and he would tell them his questions. What, she wondered, was so significant about those questions.

She turned away from the door and walked back into the flat, leaving him to enter uninvited yet still technically trespassing. She would first hear his questions — there would still be time enough to call the police.

Simon stepped inside, closed the door and followed her into the living-room where he stood very still and watched as Rachel made a big production of pouring herself a drink, lighting a cigarette and settling herself on the settee. In retaliation he took his time about lighting a cigar, deliberately giving her more time to ponder his intentions.

At last she spoke. 'Well?'

'Tell me about Wilkie,' he said.

'I already did.'

'So you did,' Simon agreed, 'but you told me too little because you were scared stiff of his client. I let you off the hook then because you were so frightened, but since then my office and flat have been wrecked and I've been 'worked over' — all as a warning to 'keep off the grass'.'

'Then keep off the damned grass,' she retorted.

'Which grass, Rachel?' he demanded softly.

She changed that subject quickly. 'Were you badly hurt?' she asked with a feigned indifference.

'A few battered ribs.'

'Painful?'

'Very.'

Rachel smiled sneeringly. 'My compliments to the chef,' she said acidly.

'It was effective,' Simon admitted, 'but clumsily executed.'

'*This* is all you came to do?' Rachel demanded. 'Just repeat your pointless enquiry about this man Wilkie and tell me how, at last, someone has caught up with you?'

'No. I've told you about the heavies just to show you the kind of people you're mixed up with,' Simon explained. 'Wilkie works for them and they don't trust you for some reason, so they have Wilkie watch you. When I came up here all that time ago to ask you about the Tronas Corporation and City-special, you talked a devil of a lot and told me nothing. When I left, Wilkie came here and questioned you about what had passed between us. You managed to assure him you'd put me off, but you know and I know that the people behind him trust no one and nothing.

'They thought their best bet was to draw my attention away so they had Wilkie slip the word to Marion that I had been having an affaire with you — and they warned you to go along with that lie. My marriage — or rather my daughter's wellbeing — meant a lot to me so I unwittingly played their game, went on the defensive and gave all my attention to resisting the divorce.

'In the end, of course, the decree nisi has been granted and I've had to accept the inevitable. Mind you.' Simon broke off to give an ironic chuckle, 'I've come to realize that it's not only inevitable but desirable — but that's by the way.

Someone started me thinking about the beginning of it all and I decided to come and see you again. Soon afterwards I was leant on and warned off the 'local dollies'.

'I couldn't figure it out at first, but coming to see you the other evening was the cause of this new pressure on me. When I came here *that* time I wasn't interested in Tronas Corporation but somebody thought I was and I was kicked around a bit. I want to know who's behind this, what it's all about, and who's using Wilkie!'

Rachel's face was expressionless, the anger was gone and so was the feigned indifference to his quest. Her eyes showed the depth of her fear, but she still had courage.

'Why d'you have to pick on me?' she demanded.

'You hold the key to all this,' he replied. 'Why the devil shouldn't I ask you?'

'I repeat my original theme — Go to the devil!'

Simon pursed his lips in a mime of deep thought, then he asked, 'Mind if I use your phone?'

'British Telecom provide phone-booths for public use — ' she replied — 'outside!'

'True,' Simon agreed reasonably, 'but that means I'd have to go out and Vincent would only insist I return here with him.'

'Vincent?'

'Come off it, Rachel,' Simon jeered. 'He's the CID man who's so interested in my case.'

'So what?' she retorted. 'What interest can he have in me?'

'He wants to know why I was worked over and how Stan Wilkie fits into this.'

'Wilkie is working for a man named Rhodes,' she offered, suddenly. Too suddenly for Simon's taste.

'That's no answer and you know it,' he snapped. 'Rhodes is a red herring!'

'What else d'you want?' she cried.

'A clue! Vincent is looking for a genuine clue, not a false trail. I've not told him everything — I've been hiding behind business confidentiality — but it seems to me I'm protecting the wrong people, so unless I get something really substantial from you I may just throw open my records and turn him loose!'

'There are people in this world who can make quite a mess of a girl who talks out of turn,' Rachel said, and set Simon thinking that she could be weakening.

'So don't talk too much. Vincent has a damned great criminal records office he can bleed for information. He won't need much more than a sniff. Either I turn him loose on my records and you get caught up as an accessory in the resultant furore or you give me a hint now and I forget to mention your connection. It doesn't matter to me any more — either way, I win!'

'You're a vicious swine, Shelley!'

'Not really,' he returned equably, 'but I could be, very easily.'

'I daren't tell you much,' Rachel whispered.

'I don't ask for much,' he encouraged.

'Just a lead,' she agreed after more careful thought. 'You're going to have to dig for what you really need. If you went in too directly they'd know I was the one who fed you the clue and I'd wind up with a face full of razor cuts.'

'Give me the lead,' Simon urged. 'If it

gets me forward I'll forget about you. But if anything goes sour, I'll remember you and I'll be back — with the police.'

'You do that, Shelley,' Rachel snapped, a bare step from hysteria. 'Now get out and leave me in peace!'

'The clue first,' he insisted.

'Oh yes.' Rachel took a firm hold on herself and smiled. It was a hard smile without warmth and smeared by a cynical sneer. 'You'll just love this,' she said maliciously. 'The clue is: Angela Whitney.'

She sensed his mental shock and laughed him from her flat, the synthetic victory serving to steady her nerves and bolster her crumbling ego.

\*  \*  \*

Through the glass panes of the partition dividing his office from the showroom, Henry Rhodes could see clearly that his caller was Simon Shelley and he glowered anxiously as he wondered what was to come next. Elaine had come home in the small hours, and he was convinced she had been with Shelley, his big dilemma was the interpretation of the term 'been with', but his mind had him suspect the worst and that angered him. And yet, paradoxically, he was honest enough to admit that his own attitudes might well have contributed by driving her into Shelley's arms. Elaine had subtly changed, she was more poised, less self-conscious in the presence of men, and the change reminded him of how Clair had become more self-assured after their honeymoon had given her her first taste of the intimate side of marriage.

The young assistant, Todd, having informed Rhodes of his caller had withdrawn into the showroom where he held himself aloof from Simon and pondered the phenomenon of his employer's failure to put on the ingratiating smile and come fawning into the shop.

Henry, in his turn, pondered upon what to do with Shelley. He was reluctant to risk any discussion in the shop and yet he was equally reluctant to introduce his 'enemy' to the more private office upstairs. He gave a mental shrug in recognition of his indecision and went into the showroom.

'Well?' he demanded bluntly.

Simon smiled disarmingly. 'I'd like an address.'

Henry's eyes narrowed suspiciously.

'Whose?'

'Jean Alcott's.'

'You have your brass nerve!' snorted Henry.

'True,' Simon acknowledged briefly. 'Now, what about that address?'

Henry made an intent study of Simon's expression where the smile remained on the face but the lips and eyes told a different story of determination. 'I don't have it,' Henry snapped. 'And, if I did, why do you need it?'

'This is business,' Simon replied. 'You wouldn't really expect me to be in breach of confidence, now would you?'

'Confidence!' snorted Henry. 'So much hogwash! But, if you really want that address you'll have to ask Mrs Shelley at Beaver's.' Henry turned away, curtly washing his hands of the matter, and stalked back to the glass paned office cubicle.

Simon smiled cheerfully, content that he had achieved his immediate objective which was to serve notice that he had no intention of sitting back and allowing matters to take a quiet course. He was sure that Wilkie would hear of it, one way or another, and that too was a source of some satisfaction. He left the showroom at a leisurely pace and, once outside, paused to consider his best route from the shop to Beaver's. He took to the back streets, and despite his intimate knowledge of the town he was quite surprised to notice how convenient the shop was to the wholesaler's.

He entered Beaver's downstairs door and climbed the stairs to the accompaniment of the clatter of a distant typewriter. When he entered the outer office where Jean Alcott would ordinarily be seated he found the room empty and from the inner room came the sound of the typewriter being thrashed by an unpractised hand.

Marion called a weary 'Come in!' in response to his knock on the inner office door, and he went in.

'Simon!' Marion rapped angrily. 'What

the devil do you want here?'

'Jean Alcott's home address.'

'What business is it of yours?'

'I'm making inquiries on behalf of a client and it's confidential so I can't give you whys and wherefores. But I do need that address.'

'I don't see why I should help you.'

'You should help because it's purely business and has no direct bearing on our personal relationship. If you want a selfish reason, then remember that I have to pay you alimony, and if I don't do my job properly there's none to give you.' He paused, and then continued: 'Besides, Henry Rhodes told me to ask you for the address.'

'Mr Rhodes?' Marion blustered nervously. 'What business is it of his?'

'Look,' said Simon with a heavy sigh, 'I know and you know that Henry has the major holding in this company and he said I should ask you Jean Alcott's address as he didn't have it.'

'Twenty-eight Laker Street,' Marion snapped testily and returned to her typing. 'Now clear off, I'm busy and I don't owe you a thing!'

'That's true,' Simon agreed though his meaning was lost on her. He opened the door again. 'Thanks,' he said insincerely and walked out.

Outside the building Simon turned towards his office and set off at a steady pace, anxious to get on with his job now that he had an address to work on. He collected his car and drove eastward along the town's central artery, still wondering if his plan to try to link one business with another until he found the combination which pointed to the source of his troubles was the right one.

He pondered the so-called clue given him by Rachel Fuhrmann and the spite which lay behind it. Did Angela really fit into the picture? And, if so, where? She was herself in business, contracted to provide a service to a group of business-men, but had she merely acceded to a request to help a friend of one of her regular clients or had she been paid to play her part in some larger plan? The special rapport which had sprung up between them was something else — it was the original reason for bringing them together which mattered most in this context.

There was a clear proposition that Abe Rousker was involved in some way. Admittedly Abe was his friend, but: 'Well, my boy, business is business and a man has no friends in business.'

And there was the counter-proposition that Simon's business, though it involved inquiries into other companies, was no threat to Abe's affairs.

Yet Angela was somehow involved in the mess and he experienced an inner desolation because of that. To him she had seemed an oasis in a desert or a safe haven from the emotional storms which had beset him. He reached Laker Street with his spirits at a low ebb and his morale in grave danger.

Simon found number twenty-eight, parked the car and went to ring the bell. The door was opened and he was confronted with a plump but hard-featured woman having no obvious genetic connection with Jean Alcott. He pasted on a smile and asked for the girl.

The woman eyed him with intense suspicion. 'What d'you want with her?'

'Business,' Simon replied shortly.

'Are you from Beaver's?'

'No.'

The woman's face retained its hostility as she sought to weigh up the caller. At last she turned away into the house, snapping over her shoulder, 'Wait.'

Simon leant his weight against the side of the doorway and waited. The sound of women's voices reached him from inside, and then Jean Alcott came to the door.

'You?' she cried angrily as soon as she recognized him. 'You can clear off!'

'How about the twenty-five quid?' Simon angled.

'You turned me down, remember?' she sneered, but there was a softening of her tone.

'You had nothing to offer.'

'And now you believe I have?'

'Possibly.'

'I don't know,' the girl returned cagily, her mind racing to seek ways and means of squeezing more from him.

Simon turned away. 'Suit yourself,' he

said with a shrug.

'Wait!'

He halted beside his car and forced the girl to come out to him.

'Not here,' Jean hissed conspiratorially. 'That old bat doesn't miss a thing. I don't want her knowing too much.'

'A cup of coffee?' he suggested offhandedly. 'A drink?'

The girl nodded. 'The 'Custodian' is usually pretty quiet at this time of day.'

Simon knew and disliked the uninspiring pub, but she was right, it would be quiet. 'Okay,' he agreed.

'I'll get my coat.'

Jean hurried back into the house and returned wearing a beige coat and swinging an ill-matching handbag. Simon slid into his seat and leant across to release the passenger door. The girl flounced in and flopped onto the seat, slamming the door after her.

'A gentleman opens a door for a lady and sees her into her seat,' she said pointedly.

'Fortunately,' Simon returned drily, 'that let's us both out.'

He drove round the block and back onto the main street, heading east again until he could swing the car into what passed for a car-park behind the hideously painted pub with its sign of an ancient top-hatted policeman.

They left the car, entered the pub by the rear door and found a quiet corner of the saloon bar.

'Gin and tonic,' said Jean before he could ask.

Simon nodded, went up to the bar and returned with two drinks.

Jean looked at the ginger ale in his hand. 'Whisky and dry ginger?' she assumed.

When he smiled, she was satisfied to accept that as an affirmative.

'I prefer a drop of 'Mother's Ruin',' she declared bluntly. 'Don't like whisky.'

'Each to their own taste.'

'About the money — ' Jean pressed.

Simon viewed her across his glass. 'Exactly who is behind Beaver's?'

'Money first,' she insisted.

'After.' His attitude was that she was free to take it or leave it.

'Henry Rhodes has a local holding company, Wholesale Supply (Amdale) Ltd.'

'I wanted something I didn't already know,' Simon replied disappointedly.

'There's an 'A. Rousker' in it with him.'

'How much of it is Rousker's?'

She shrugged. 'Something like ten per cent.'

'Just an interest,' Simon observed.

'That's all,' the girl agreed.

'It doesn't help me much,' Simon sighed. 'Certainly not twenty-five quid's worth. Does anyone else have a finger in Wholesale Supply?'

'Another couple of holding companies I can't remember.'

'Reliance Investments?' Simon prompted.

'Er — er — no.'

'You sound uncertain,' he pressed.

'Reliance, yes; Investments, no.'

'What, then?'

'Shut up, I'm thinking!'

Simon pulled a face and gave his full attention to the ginger ale.

'Hunter-Reliance Holdings,' the girl said at last.

'Anything else?' Simon asked.

She shook her head. 'I only wish there were.'

'Oh, why?'

'Maybe I could squeeze some more money out of you!'

'Fuhrmann,' said Simon, out of the blue. 'Does that name mean anything to you?'

'It sounds German,' Jean observed. 'Yes, I've heard it before.'

'Where?'

'Another fiver?' she countered.

Simon nodded.

'I heard it mentioned when I worked for Beverington Industrial Developments as a 'Temp',' the girl explained. 'A board meeting was breaking up and the directors came streaming along a corridor. Half of them were mouthing threats against the chap Fuhrmann for throwing a spanner into some big deal.'

'Who's on the board?' he pressed. 'Anyone I know?'

'I only identified a few of them,' Jean replied with a shrug. 'Compton-Archer,

Pickersgill, Gausden, Rousker — they're all I can recall.'

'Have you anything else?'

'No. Not a thing — and you can believe that, for if I had I'd be screwing some more money out of you.'

That struck Simon as fair comment so he dropped his questioning and slipped her the money.

'You've given me a fiver over the odds,' Jean observed.

Simon grinned as he stood up. 'Honest endeavour nets bonuses,' he said as he walked from the table.

\* \* \*

Amdale was once a market town and the focal point of a strong farming community, but latterly the place had degenerated to a small inland town of no note. The population had reached twenty thousand and was still rising, and of that number a fair proportion of the working people commuted to London daily. For Simon Shelley's money, they could 'keep' both Amdale and commuting.

He parked his car in the area which had once been the cattle market and set off in search of Terry's Car Hire. It was the simplest of tasks, for Walter Terry had taken over a large barn-like industrial structure beside the market in a spot where once there had been a thriving trade in farm machinery.

Terry was a small, alert man of about thirty and already balding. He signed for Simon to have a seat and then sat behind the desk to study Simon's card.

'Are you the Simon Shelley who got worked over the other night?' Terry asked.

'The same,' Simon agreed ruefully, 'and I've got the marks to prove it.' He paused before adding: 'News travels fast.'

'We get the evening papers up from Beverington,' Terry explained. 'Now, Mr Shelley, what can I do for you?'

'I'm trying to trace a furniture manufacturer,' said Simon. 'It could be either Beesuite or Alderplan. Their finished goods are sometimes delivered to Beaver's in Beverington in vans hired from you.'

'We have standing hire arrangements

with various small firms,' Terry hedged apologetically. 'I don't concern myself with the detail of what they do.'

Simon grinned. It was obvious that Terry wouldn't talk — either through loyalty to his customers or because someone's tentacles reached a long way. He shrugged, it wasn't the end of the world. 'I understand,' he said and rose to leave.

Terry also rose quickly, produced a cigar case and offered Simon a conciliatory cigar, but Simon shook his head in refusal. 'I really am sorry,' Terry said, 'I'd like to help you after that beating-up. I can't stick these hard men who imagine a heavy boot makes them right.'

Simon walked from the office onto the forecourt where he halted, took out his own cigars and took great pains to light one in front of Terry who was watching him from the office window.

He found 'P. T. Baker, Furniture Manufacturer', far up a side-street in a newish structure erected on what had once been railway sidings before Britain decided that the best way to attract people to use railways was to take away said railways.

The receptionist-cum-typist regretted the absence of Mr Baker, and could she help?

'I represent a new retail outlet for furniture,' Simon lied cheerfully. 'I hear excellent reports of your Beesuite and Alderplan lines.'

'Sorry,' the girl interrupted, smiling regretfully. 'We are at full production capacity already and our entire output is wholesaled through Beaver's of Beverington. You'd have to talk to them.'

'How about your parent company?' Simon wondered innocently.

He caught the girl off guard. 'Kerry, Bissall?' she hooted derisively. 'The only things *they* make are raids on our profits!' Then she realized her error and checked any further outburst.

'It's okay,' Simon reassured her, 'I didn't hear that. In any case, my only interest is in furniture, not in 'who's taken over what'.'

The girl looked about her quickly. 'They've not taken us over, exactly,' she explained confidentially, 'but they helped Mr Baker build up the business. He likes to let people believe he did it all himself. Still, to get back to business; would you like me to jot down Beaver's address for you?'

Simon said he'd appreciate that and allowed her to go through with it. He gave her a beaming smile of thanks and left the building.

Walking back to the High Street, he considered what he had gained: the names of three firms, but they told him little, he would have to check further on their doings to see what else he could learn of their connections.

His next call was on Erwin Rogers, a tall, studious sort of young man who wore a permanent frown of concentration.

'Your family business in Beverington,' Simon opened when the introductions were done and Rogers had handed over to his eighteen-year-old girl assistant with an injunction to ensure that the antiques did not walk off on their own.

Rogers shook his head of fully liberated hair. 'There's nothing to tell,' he said. 'We sold up and got out.'

'Henry Rhodes bought you out?' Simon suggested.

'Well,' Rogers replied with a shrug, 'I suppose so. Actually the firm was Beaver (Wholesale) Limited, but I think it amounts to the same thing. Our old business had gone flat and become a total bind, I wanted out.'

'But Beaver's isn't really Beaver's,' Simon asserted more boldly than he privately considered justified. 'I need to speak to the fountain head.'

'You and me, both,' Rogers growled feelingly. 'At first I thought that Henry Rhodes was Beaver. He is in so far as he holds the leading position on what passes for their board of directors, but I have it on the grapevine that it's a delegated post.'

'Rousker?' Simon tossed into the pot.

Rogers shrugged. 'Another appointee,' he sighed. 'He has to be, for he and Rhodes are like oil and water, they'd never work together voluntarily.'

'Who appointed Rousker?' Simon pressed.

'I'm not certain.'

'Then guess,' Simon urged. 'How about Kerry, Bissall?'

'It's on the cards. It's impossible to say, really. Kerry, Bissall is just a name, another holding company. I tried to look them up once — their office is in a down-at-heel stone shanty in the City. Just a sign on the door of a one-room 'suite' of offices, and I'll swear that room was empty.'

'What's your connection with P. T. Baker?' Simon tried next.

Rogers shrugged. 'There's no secret,' he returned openly, 'it's timber. Antiques are my line, but in this game I get wind of sell-ups and demolitions. I buy antiques, demolition timber and property for demolition. I take what I can sell and Baker's have the pick of the wood. You'd be surprised at the economics.'

'Don't doubt I would,' Simon agreed. He paused long enough to give Rogers a look to show he found the dealer an honest man. He took a breath. 'Rachel Fuhrmann?'

Rogers shuddered involuntarily. 'I'd

like to know her game,' he said feelingly.

'I thought that was obvious,' Simon suggested, grinning.

'Don't you believe it!' Rogers scoffed. 'That girl's main fortune lies in what she knows of certain business deals, not in the body that God gave her.'

'What deals are these?' Simon pressed.

Rogers' frown deepened. 'I don't know enough to be able to give you chapter and verse. Maybe they involve Kerry, Bissall; maybe it's City-special (Holdings) Limited; maybe it's anyone.'

'What about City-special?'

Rogers shook his head. 'Someone was talking about a connection between Rachel and City-special. She knew something about a deal and he didn't like it.'

'Who was this 'someone'?'

'A man named Wilkie.'

'And how did you come to hear the exchanges?' Simon demanded.

'I was to meet Rousker, and when I turned up early Wilkie was with him.'

# 11

Jack Scott showed the young woman to a chair and walked round his desk to sit in the leather-covered swivel chair. 'I'd like to say this right away, Miss Rhodes,' he said. 'I find it highly unusual for a young woman to employ a detective to investigate her own father and his associates, and I think I'd like an explanation of some sort — there are certain areas where I draw a very definite line.'

'Please don't mistake my motives, Mr Scott,' Elaine replied earnestly. 'I phoned you to make this investigation only because certain events have made me suspect that my father may be into something away over his head and, perhaps, be unaware of his predicament.'

Scott studied her with great care. He was an ex-Metropolitan policeman and considered he was a fair judge of people. Elaine seemed straight enough. Her cheque had arrived promptly after her call and he'd made considerable headway with preliminary inquiries. He decided to tell her what he knew.

'Your father has, in general, done what he has always led you to believe he has done,' he reported. 'His course in London has been clear and regular. He comes up on the first train from Beverington, does the rounds of a set group of wholesale businesses and warehouses, spends the night in town, visits one or two more business premises on the following morning and catches an early afternoon train home. He is so regular that his contacts reckon you could set your watch by him.'

Elaine's expression showed only polite interest — no surprise, no disappointment.

Scott continued: 'I'll let you have a detailed report if — '

'His hotel?' Elaine cut in.

'Which?'

'That's what I'd like to know,' said Elaine.

He smiled apologetically. 'I'm afraid I don't know that yet,' Scott regretted.

'Your father was once accustomed to making regular use of one small hotel in Kensington but he hasn't been seen there for a couple of years.'

'Then where *does* he stay?'

Scott shook his head. 'I can't say — yet.'

'But you will,' Elaine declared.

'Look, Miss Rhodes,' he asked cautiously, 'are you *sure* you wish to know?'

'My wishes are beside the point,' she returned. 'I need to know exactly what is going on, and if there's anything of an embarrassing nature about it then I want to hear that, too. Now, why the caution?'

'When your father stayed at that hotel,' Scott said, 'he was generally accompanied by a young woman.'

'D'you think he may have set her up somewhere?' Elaine pressed.

'Possibly,' he agreed, 'but I doubt it. He's rumoured to be associating with a girl named Mira Feaney. She's part Irish.'

'This Mira Feaney is the girl he used to take to the hotel?' Elaine guessed.

'No.'

'So he has had more than one,' Elaine

observed, struggling desperately to sustain a façade of sophistication. She felt that she should have been more hurt than she was at discovering her father's infidelity to her mother, but her own recent experiences had blurred the demarkation lines between good and bad, right and wrong in the sexual field.

'He's kept to only one girl at a time,' Scott explained. 'The girl at the hotel was of German origin — Rachel Fuhrmann — and she later took a flat where, I'm told, he visited her fairly regularly. He may have been keeping her, but I doubt that, the economics of such an arrangement would be too heavy an additional burden. I know that Rachel Fuhrmann retired some months later when she seemed to be the focus of a 'protection' problem. Your father appears to have looked around for a while and then found this Feaney woman.'

'All this will be in your detailed report?'

'Yes, Miss.'

Elaine was thoughtful for a while before asking, 'What d'you make of my father?'

Scott moved uncomfortably in his chair. 'You're employing me to do a job,' he said, 'but, to be honest, I'm not happy about it. I'd dread the prospect of my own daughter mistrusting me to such a degree.'

'I *don't* mistrust my father,' Elaine insisted. 'At least, not in the sense you mean. He seems to have set out to destroy my faith in a young man and all for reasons too obscure to discover.'

'You want a lever to get him off your back, is that it?'

'I want to know why he's gone to the extremes he has,' she returned. 'His reaction has been too forceful to be accounted for simply.'

'Do you imagine the Feaney woman is concerned?'

'Her or Rachel Fuhrmann,' Elaine agreed, pulling a face. 'Either association could fill him with a sense of guilt which he is trying to allay by giving a heavy response to my own association. The difference is that I am single and, as you can see, properly of age — and more — while he has an ailing wife. To be honest, though, I suspect some sort of business motive.'

'Business?' Scott doubted.

'My friend investigates businesses.'

'And your father — by your guess — resents this man's prying into a sensitive area of business?'

'That's what I think, yes.'

'Have you anything to go on — other than intuition?'

'You mentioned Rachel Fuhrmann. She seems to tie in with my friend, my father and a private detective named Wilkie.'

Scott sat forward eagerly. 'Stan Wilkie, eh?' he asked, his interest caught and held.

'D'you know him?' asked Elaine. 'He seems a violent sort of person.'

'It was once my privilege to pinch him on a GBH charge,' explained Scott with some relish. 'We made the charge stick, and after that he kept off the rough stuff with anyone who seemed likely to have the guts to complain to the police. In general he put in a proxy if someone needed a little pressure.'

'You don't like him,' Elaine observed
drily.

'Does anyone?'

'Certainly not my friend.'

'Oh?'

'He was beaten up the other evening by
two men who, he swears, spoke with
south London accents.'

'It's your guess that Wilkie's behind it,'
Scott assumed. 'It's certainly typical of
him. D'you have any idea who Wilkie's
working for?'

'My father, for one.'

'For what purpose? Investigating your
friend?'

'Yes.'

'Who is your friend?'

'I'm sorry — ' she regretted.

'Suit yourself,' Scott said, sitting back
in his chair and reaching for a foolscap
envelope, 'but you'd better hire yourself
another detective.' He tossed the envelope
across the desk. 'My report,' he said.
'You've paid for it.'

'But — ' Elaine began, nonplussed
— 'but why?'

'It's a matter of trust, Miss,' he

explained. 'I'm an ex-copper and I like to have *all* the relevant information on a case. Without that name, I quit!'

Elaine stared at the envelope and considered the position. She badly wanted to get to the bottom of the business, and her attempt to approach the problem from a fresh angle seemed doomed because she wanted to screen Simon. At last she gave a resigned shrug. 'Simon Shelley,' she breathed.

★   ★   ★

Simon entered the first-floor office above a small Co-op grocery in Amdale High Street. The girl behind the desk glanced up with half-hearted interest. 'May I help you?'

Simon assured her she could and added: 'Stan Wilkie, please.'

'D'you have an appointment?'

'No.'

'Well, I'm afraid Mr Wilkie is very busy.'

'Tell him Simon Shelley is here.'

'Sorry,' she said without an ounce of sincerity.

'Tell him!' Simon grated ominously.

She threw him a look bordering on defiance but met only the cold determination in his eyes. She shrugged, picked up the intercom handset and said, 'There's a Simon Shelley for you. He doesn't have an appointment but he seems to imagine that doesn't matter — Okay, I'll tell him.'

The girl replaced the receiver, tossed a glare of irritation at Simon and said, 'You'll have to wait.'

Simon took a chair in a corner of the room from which position he could see both doors and the receptionist/secretary. One thing he would say for her, she looked good — except for a certain surliness which he doubted derived from their recent clash. She was not local, her voice had a harsh London whine.

He lit a cigar and had smoked for five minutes when the inner office door opened and Henry Rhodes emerged, red faced, angry and apprehensive.

Rhodes closed the door quickly and hurried across the room to Simon. 'Go home, man!' he hissed. 'In the name of

God, go!' He straightened up, turned and, after casting a glance at the inner door, left the premises.

Simon, duly impressed by the power of Rhodes' performance, wondered at the man's ubiquity, and only afterwards concerned himself with the reason for the injunction. The question was whether Henry had tried to warn him of impending trouble or to drive him away before he could foul up some business scheme.

'You can go in now,' the girl said, jerking him out of his reverie.

He nodded, rose slowly and moved unhurriedly to the door into Wilkie's room.

The man was on his feet, big, powerful and anxious to impress Simon with his physique. 'Hello, Shelley,' he said.

Simon nodded by way of greeting and took in what he saw. The latent power of the man was obvious, and even the signs of advancing years were insignificant against that.

'I heard about your accident,' said Wilkie.

'No accident,' Simon returned offhand-edly. 'Your boys get full marks for trying.'

'Mine?' Wilkie even managed to look hurt.

'Your hired muscle, imported to warn me off the scent of some funny business afoot locally.'

'Me?' Wilkie scoffed. 'Hire 'heavies'? Do I *look* the kind of man who needs to hire anyone to do that kind of thing?'

'No,' Simon conceded, 'you don't, but then looks have nothing to do with this. You hired those blokes so you couldn't be accused.'

'I could mash you with one hand,' Wilkie averred without bombast.

'Probably,' Simon agreed, dismissing the matter as of no consequence. 'The point is that you *won't* do it. You tried the heavy hand once too often and the victim went to the police. The result was that you were nailed on a charge of grievous bodily harm and now you only use the strong arm by proxy.'

Wilkie's face wore a hurt smile, and even his eyes showed no malice. 'You slander me,' he observed sadly.

'Sue!'

The hurt smile broadened into an appreciative grin. 'You're a cheeky perisher,' Wilkie acknowledged. He gestured for Simon to sit in the 'client's chair' and almost offered him a cigarette before realizing Simon still held the smouldering panatella.

Wilkie took a cigarette for himself, lit it and sank heavily into a handsome leather-covered swivel chair. 'What brings you here?'

Simon looked at him squarely. 'I want information,' he said bluntly. 'I want you to tell me who you're working for.'

Wilkie's eyebrows lifted in amused incredulity. 'Oh! Come off it, squire,' he protested. 'We're in a similar line of business, you and I. I don't divulge confidences and I certainly don't name clients!'

'We're *not* in the same line of business,' Simon countered. 'I investigate only business matters.'

'The principles apply equally,' Wilkie returned, unmoved.

'Henry Rhodes just walked out of here,'

Simon went on, firing speculatively in the dark. 'He told you there was to be no further investigation of me and to cut out the harassment. Of course you could accept the direction if Henry was the only interested party, but you and I know that wrecking my office and working me over had nothing to do with what Henry believed you were doing on his behalf.'

Wilkie's smile persisted though there was a small but noticeable gathering of his brows. 'Just suppose — purely for argument's sake — ' he said slowly, 'that I did hire a couple of heavies to rough up your place and leave marks on you, why would I do that?'

'Rachel Fuhrmann.'

'That old boot?' Wilkie hooted derisively. 'Now why the devil would I go to such lengths for her? — Assuming that I did!'

'The verbal warning that preceded the boots told me to stay away from the birds,' Simon explained. 'It was couched in general terms and it would be easy for me to tell the police I suspected Henry Rhodes' hand in the affair. That would have torpedoed him if he'd really been your main client so, if you were willing to sell him down the river, there has to be someone else behind it; someone far more important; someone afraid of what I might learn from Rachel Fuhrmann. The warning was really for me to stay away from *her*, not Elaine Rhodes.'

Wilkie relaxed noticeably; he leant back against the deep padding of the black high-backed chair. It was a big chair and it took up the whole mass of the man. He drew on his cigarette. 'I don't doubt,' he said amusedly, 'that you're a dab hand at angling but in this case you're fishing in tainted water.'

'Tainted?'

'Yes. 'Taint yours to fish in!'

'Ah! But I think it is,' Simon retorted.

'You do?' said Wilkie in mock astonishment. 'Now why would you imagine that, I wonder?'

'I'm learning so much about the pond, you see,' Simon returned, going along with the analogy. 'The big fish, the little fish, the ones which put up a good fight when hooked, and those which give up easily. However, it's the pike that I'm after. I've never seen it but I know it's there. It's rather a big one for such a small pool, greedy and as ferocious as any of its kind. This big fish has already interfered with my fishing, scaring off many of the other fish, and I reckon I have a right to try for it.'

'Shelley,' Wilkie chuckled throatily, 'you kill me!'

'Months ago,' Simon continued explanatorily, 'I was asked by a client to look into a firm called City-special (Holdings) and very early on I realized that Rachel Fuhrmann had some important but obscure connection with them. I went to see her and we talked long and hard. You — or one of your hirelings — were also keeping an eye on Rachel. You saw me, reported my presence and quest to your principals and they, afraid I might blow open some scheme of theirs, looked for a way to divert me from the investigation but to do so without arousing my suspicion. My marriage and family were my most vulnerable area so they struck there. This shows that I was pretty well known and understood by your principals.'

'Interesting tale that,' Wilkie mused. 'You should get someone to set it to music — as a film it would do better business than the 'Sound of Music'.'

Simon shrugged. 'The chicken are about to come home to roost,' he said. 'The police have picked up your heavies and it's just a matter of time before they come for you.'

Wilkie's grin broadened and he seemed totally unimpressed. 'You seem to be obsessed with the fantasy that I engineered this attack on you,' he said blandly, 'when in fact you probably had it coming to you from innumerable sources and motives. That's one thing you and I really do have in common — we collect enemies like a dog collects fleas.'

'It was you all right,' Simon averred, equally unmoved, 'acting on the orders of someone far cleverer and with so much more to lose than anyone else. You can make life easier for yourself by giving me their name or even a simple clue to them. Keep silent and you can go under with them when I demolish their business structure. I can do it and you'd better believe that!'

'You're bluffing,' Wilkie sneered confidently. 'You've got nothing or you wouldn't have bothered to come here.'

'Suit yourself,' Simon replied with a shrug of dismissal. 'Just so long as you don't mind being charged with those two apes who beat me up; so long as you don't mind being tied in with a London prostitution racket; and so long as you don't mind the revenge your principals will undoubtedly bring down on your head.'

'If you could keep a straight face, Shelley,' Wilkie returned affably, 'you'd be a whizz at poker — that's ninety-nine per cent bluff with a worthless hand!'

'Of course,' Simon added by way of postscript as he moved towards the door, 'there is that detective constable by the name of Vincent — a quiet, personable, persistent chap who's been pressing me for a lead. It's very possible he may be interested in what brought you down this way from London.' Without a backward glance he walked out.

# 12

Simon was driving sedately towards Beverington when a Mini took station behind him and stayed there despite many opportunities to pass. The driver was unrecognizable behind Sundym glass, but it was plain that he was tailing Simon who was quite content to allow him to stay there. Vaguely Simon wondered why Wilkie would send a palpably tiro to do such a job.

When he reached his office, Simon ran the car into the one-time stable at the rear and was about to close the garage doors when the Mini Clubman inched into the small square of cobbled yard. Simon sighed — he had no particular fancy for another beating. He stepped close to his car and reached into the window to retrieve a handy tyre lever he had slipped into the glove pocket as additional insurance.

The girl who stepped apprehensively

from the Mini looked very far from aggressive. She was Wilkie's receptionist and her expression was sufficient to tell Simon he wouldn't need the tyre lever.

'You wanted to talk to me?' he asked, keeping his voice casual.

'Yes,' she agreed throatily, 'please.'

'Come into the office,' Simon suggested.

'No.' The girl darted furtive glances about the yard as though fearful that some ogre was about to leap out at her. 'Here. Now. I have to go quickly.'

Simon nodded. 'Okay,' he agreed. 'Say what you have to say.'

'Wilkie's on a blackmail case.'

'Who?'

'Rachel Fuhrmann.'

'The victim?' Simon doubted.

'No! The blackmailer!'

'Then who's the victim?'

'Sorry,' she said, 'that's confidential.'

'For God's sake!' Simon snorted. 'You've already broken one confidence!'

'Yeah, but there are limits, see?' The girl began to get back into the Mini.

'He's worked you over?' Simon guessed.

The girl's head came to the open window for her to say: 'But he leaves no marks that show.'

Simon let himself into his office while his mind was wondering why Wilkie had sent the girl after him with her tiny piece of information. Wilkie appeared to be covering himself by having the girl deliver the lead as coming from herself. If his principals caught up with him he could then make a convincing case against the girl. If the scenario was the correct one, why was Wilkie doing it at all?

Conjecture would get him nowhere at that stage. Wilkie's motives were of far less immediate moment than the actual information.

Simon sat down at the desk, swivelled the chair round to his card index file and began selecting file-cards: Ronas; City-special; Kerry, Bissall; P. T. Baker; Terry Car & Van Hire; Beaver; Hunter-Reliance; Beverington Industrial.

When those were complete he dug into

the personal files: Fuhrmann; Compton-Archer; Pickersgill; Gausden; Rhodes; Rousker.

It had been Sir Charles Compton-Archer who had first asked him to investigate Ronas and City-special and who had suggested that he should include Rachel Fuhrmann in his itinerary. The question now before him was: Was Sir Charles genuinely seeking his help or setting him up?

On the face of things, Compton-Archer had nothing personal to gain from lumbering him with a divorce. Indeed, Sir Charles's anger had been perfectly genuine when he learned that Simon had been giving more attention to his private rearguard action than to business. So who else could have felt threatened?

Simon accepted that there were two common factors — Rachel Fuhrmann and Abe Rousker. Abe had also arranged his 'consolation' visit to Angela Whitney. Opposite Angela's flat lived Mira Feaney on whom Henry Rhodes was a regular caller. Henry and Abe had a common interest at Beaver's. And, Rachel had tossed into the pot Angela's name.

He lit a cigar and began building 'family trees' based upon the filecards he had before him, adding to them by frequent cross-reference.

He was so engrossed that he failed to hear Elaine Rhodes enter, and she was at his side before he became aware of her perfume. He stood up, held her and kissed her.

'How're you feeling now?' she asked solicitously.

Simon gave her a squeeze and kissed her again. 'Much better,' he replied.

'That's not what I meant,' she chided gently.

'Ah, but I did,' he returned gallantly.

'How about your bruises?' Elaine pressed.

'Improving by the minute.'

Elaine took a moment to glance meaningly at the cluttered desk. 'You're busy,' she observed enquiringly.

Simon smiled: 'I've found a common denominator,' he explained.

'Really?'

'Rachel Fuhrmann.'

At once her face fell into a serious expression. 'My father has been associated with her, Simon.'

'Your father? Where? When?'

'A London hotel, a year or more back. I have the report of a private detective.' Elaine fished in her bag pulled out Jack Scott's report and handed it to him.

Simon studied the envelope uncertainly. 'You don't mind if I read it?' he asked hesitantly.

'Have you had tea?' Elaine cut in, apparently ignoring his question.

'No.'

'Then I'll go up to the flat and prepare it,' she announced, 'while you read the report.'

\* \* \*

Simon chewed purposefully into hot buttered toast which his jaded mind registered as unpalatable flannelette. There was nothing wrong with the food, and his apparent distaste was no reflection upon Elaine's efforts, but he

270

simply seemed incapable of enjoying any food just then.

'What d'you make of the report?' Elaine asked as she poured the tea.

Simon swallowed and gazed at her sadly. 'I'm afraid,' he said, 'your father's been taken for a sucker.'

'The reverse,' she protested, 'surely?'

He shook his head. 'No,' he insisted. 'My game of 'Snap' downstairs, when related to this fellow Scott's report and a few things I've picked up, suggests to me that your father's small initial indiscretions have led him into parting with shares in his own companies as 'gifts' to his lady friends — notably Rachel Fuhrmann in the past and, in all probability, Mira Feaney more recently.'

'You mean to say that Rachel owns large blocks of shares in father's companies?'

'Oddly enough,' said Simon, 'no, I don't.'

'Then what?'

'I believe she was employed as a prostitute by a business concern and she was directed to suggest that her clients who felt they wished to make her little gifts should make over to her a few shares. Those shares were then passed over to her controlling company. By encouraging her customers to believe she regarded each of them as her favourite, she could — over a lengthy period — acquire some quite sizeable holdings for her principals. If the client was a man in business of about the same calibre as your father, it's possible she could dictate quite a lot of policy, too.'

'But,' Elaine asked, puzzled, 'what about the Feaney girl now that Rachel is no longer my father's companion?'

'I think she may be employed by the same group,' Simon guessed, 'and be doing the same sort of thing for them.'

'And Rachel?'

'She was thrown out of the organization because she began to get greedy and was taking in 'outsiders' unknown to her principals and creaming some shares off them. Rachel then stayed out of the game in London but came down here where she felt strong enough and free enough to try a little business manipulation; a little blackmail; and quite some sexual persuasion.'

'Then she could be putting pressure on my father?'

'He doesn't yield to pressure,' Simon said, 'remember?'

'No,' she agreed, 'he doesn't, does he. How about Mira Feaney? Could she be trying something?'

Simon shrugged. 'It's possible.'

'Jack Scott hasn't yet been able to trace her address,' Elaine regretted.

'But I know it, I told you about seeing him in London.'

'Of course.' Elaine could justifiably have pressed for more details but she had the good sense to realise that whatever Simon had been doing before she had gone to bed with him was his business and demanding chapter and verse could too easily destroy her new-found happiness.

They finished the tea and washed up, then Elaine came into his arms in search of reassurance. They kissed, the intensity increasing rapidly until the outcome was inevitable.

'You're sure you want this?' Simon asked. 'Sarah may call and catch her teacher in flagrante delicto.'

'Homework,' Elaine whispered confidently, 'will tie her to the house. It has to be now,' she added. 'I *must* be at home tonight.'

Simon's hands were already busy at the buttons of her blouse, and she smiled up at him. What did the past matter to her? She wanted him now and he wanted her, what else was there?

★  ★  ★

Becky Rousker opened her front door and saw Simon Shelley standing inside the open-fronted porch. She stepped back, smiled a welcome and waved him inside.

'Simon!' she exclaimed delightedly. 'My dear boy. Come in, come in! I'm afraid Abe's not at home just now but he should be back at some time this evening.' She closed the door behind him and ushered him into the lounge where, without preamble, she poured him a drink.

Feeling strangely ill at ease in this home

of friends, Simon was hard put to it to decide what to say. In the end he said virtually nothing. 'I'd've liked to have seen Abe,' was the best he could manage.

'Would it be any good giving me a message for him?' Becky suggested, passing him the drink and wearing a frown of puzzlement at Simon's transparent uncertainty.

He sipped the whisky and sank into an easy-chair. 'I don't like what I've got into, Becky,' he said.

'What *are* you into, my dear boy?' she asked, resting on the arm of the settee. 'Come along, explain to mama.'

Simon sighed heavily and began. 'I became interested to know why Stan Wilkie, an ex-London private detective would shop me to my wife. Why he would tell her I had been unfaithful with Rachel Fuhrmann when he knew damned well that I hadn't.'

'So Marion fancied someone else and had this Wilkie keep an eye on you in the hope you'd make a mistake,' Becky decided with a shrug.

With a shake of his head, Simon began

a tale. 'No,' he said decisively. 'Marion had no one in mind at that time and she had precious little money — certainly not enough to pay a man like Wilkie. The truth is that he was working for a group of London businesses which, coincidentally, has strong local connections and his actual assignment was to watch Rachel Fuhrmann, and to report back on all her visitors and activities. He reported back and was told to offer my wife 'evidence' of my infidelity — the object being to put me on the defensive.'

Becky moved from the arm to the seat of the settee. 'Why would they — the businessmen — do that?' she posed. 'Why try to divert you?'

'I was investigating two businesses: Ronas, and City-special on behalf of a local businessman, with particular orders to check on Rachel Fuhrmann's connections with them. The object of getting me involved in a domestic problem was to pull my mind off Rachel, Ronas and City-special. It worked fine. I let the job slide and, in due course, lost it. I didn't realize at the time — but I do now — that whoever is behind Wilkie knows me well, so well that they could count upon my love for my daughter Sarah making me fight with everything I possessed to continue to be a father to her in more than just name.'

'I gather from this that you have concluded that Abe is the villain of this piece.'

'You gather wrongly,' Simon returned. 'I find it difficult to see him in the leading rôle in this but, wittingly or unwittingly, he is deeply involved. I like Abe and I take no pleasure from casting him with the 'bad guys' and I'd like to give him every opportunity to change sides before I demolish the pyramid of businesses and holding companies which he supports and which may control him.'

'Now why on earth,' Becky wondered, 'would you wish to destroy legitimate businesses?'

'Revenge,' Simon declared unrepentantly. 'Pure bloody-minded revenge and nothing more. They set out to destroy my marriage. They laid down the ground rules and I'm going to play to those rules.'

'But you can't destroy a business empire — even a small one — as easily as that,' Becky cried, her brow deeply furrowed by her concern. 'You, Simon, of all people should know that. All you'd do is bring down some little fellow, like Abe, and that would make it an act of petty spite, not a major act of retribution. Let it drop — for your own sake as well as Abe and those like him.'

'I'm sorry.' Simon shook his head sadly. 'All I can do for Abe is what I'm doing now — giving him the chance to get out from under.'

'Well, when he comes in I'll tell him,' Becky returned, hurt. 'If he wants to talk to you, where will you be?'

'Tonight, at home. Tomorrow, I'll be in London beginning my demolition job.'

'Why London?'

'Two reasons. First, I've been given the name of someone in London who may know something but not be aware of that knowledge. Second, Wilkie is a London man.'

'Only the other day you were worked over for prying into things which someone considered didn't concern you,' Becky reminded him pointedly. 'You could find it a lot worse in London, that's where the big boys play.'

'It won't matter to that extent,' Simon replied with a shrug of indifference. 'I've left word with my solicitors that if I catch another thrashing or die — from whatever cause — they are to hand to the police my full report and findings on this affair. I'll take my chances on the outcome,' he concluded.

Simon got to his feet and moved towards the door. Becky Rousker rose to see him out. Without looking back at her, he said: 'Pull Abe out of it, Becky. Now, before it's too late.'

★   ★   ★

Henry Rhodes followed his daughter into the living-room of their home. His wife had already retired for the night and they were free to talk.

Elaine halted and tossed Jack Scott's

report onto the coffee-table with a challenging gesture.

'What's this?' Henry demanded.

'Read it, Father,' she snapped.

'Tell me why — ' he began.

'Read it!' she cut in coldly.

He glared at her, angry and hurt that the daughter he loved so dearly could speak to him so. Elaine's gaze met his, the gleam in her eyes showing no repentance and no intention to tolerate a refusal. He sat down in his favourite chair, took the report from the envelope and began reading.

Elaine walked to another chair, sat down and waited patiently.

After a time Henry came to the end of the report. He folded the typewritten sheets and replaced them in the envelope with meticulous care. 'I deeply resent,' he declared regretfully, 'your having paid a man to pry into my personal affairs. Having expressed that resentment, I have to acknowledge that you may have felt you had some justification for doing so and that I may have been foolish — in the view of many people — to have become so entangled. I now assume that you propose to make some further use of this knowledge.'

'Possibly,' Elaine admitted, 'though not in the manner you undoubtedly expect.'

'You wish to use this as a lever to persuade me to stop pursuing my efforts to show you Simon Shelley in his true light?'

'No.'

'Then is it your intention to have me drop these London 'connections'?'

'No, Father. On the face of it you are being disloyal to Mother, but I have a far better understanding of your relationship than you imagine and the — er — indiscretions, if you want it put delicately, are understandable and forgivable by me, at least.'

'Then come to the point, girl!'

'I shall require your assistance.'

'In what, pray,' he demanded cautiously.

'To help Simon discover who is behind the perjured evidence which led to his divorce and, later, to his beating.'

Henry looked directly at his daughter, a

sad half-smile playing about his lips. 'Elaine, child,' he said ruefully though there was a note of affection in his voice, 'in your sweet naïveté you can't possibly know what you're asking me to do.'

'Just *what* am I asking you to do, Father?'

'Destroy myself.'

'Ridiculous,' she scoffed.

'Not so ridiculous,' Henry insisted. 'My businesses are no longer my own. If I help Shelley, the end product would be to topple a sizeable group of companies, and my small firms would go, too.'

'But how is that possible?' Elaine's doubts as to her father's veracity were as clear in her expression as in her words. 'You own your own businesses — jointly with Mother in most cases, and others jointly with me — how could the failure of others affect you, except in the normal run of business recession?'

For the first time in her life Elaine saw her father slump in utter dejection.

'It began,' he confessed, 'with Rachel Fuhrmann. At one time I was somewhat infatuated with her and we would often share a room at a Kensington hotel — just as Scott says here,' he tapped the envelope, 'but I made the mistake of making her a gift of a few of my shares. She wanted more. By various means — I'll leave that to your imagination — she coaxed, cajoled and even blackmailed more shares from me from time to time. In the end I was obliged to take over your mother's shares in order to retain a firm hold on my businesses. For my own protection — and, indirectly, your's and Clair's — I rid myself of Rachel and set about arranging a whole new group of companies, in a sense it protected me from the consequences of my own folly.

'Things improved again and I was comfortably in control once more. Then, one wet and miserable evening, I met Mira Feaney. She was very different from Rachel, kind, good humoured and truly affectionate, and again I made the mistake of handing over a few shares, and it all began again.'

'So,' Elaine observed, 'she was no better than Rachel!'

'Ah!' cried Henry, momentarily triumphant. 'But she was. I checked up on the whereabouts of those shares and found they'd gone direct to a holding company. The girl was as much their pawn as I was. I found myself trapped again by blackmail, but this time it was through the other company, not Mira. She stuck loyally to her profession.'

'So once again you're no longer in full control of your own businesses,' Elaine noted disgustedly. 'You're just a tool in the hands of someone else!'

'Yes, and on top of that, I've proved myself a fool!'

Elaine stood up and, without a word, left the room. Henry let her go, he was too full of his own woes to worry any more.

To his surprise she returned within a few minutes bearing a folder filled with documents. She tossed it onto her father's lap. 'My bank statements and so on,' she said. 'Whatever money is shown there is yours if you will use it to break out of this circle of evil now and set up fresh companies in which you and I are equal and you can do nothing about moving a single share without my prior approval.'

Henry nodded his acceptance, he was unable to speak, and Elaine saw that his eyes glistened with latent tears.

'You are going to give me all the information about the campaign against Simon,' Elaine announced. 'There must be no holding back!'

'No holding back,' he agreed. 'Then what will you do?'

'We,' she declared firmly, 'are going to speak to Detective Constable Vincent.'

# 13

Rachel Fuhrmann opened her door and looked up at the sheer bulk of her caller, but she was not overawed for he offered her no threat. She smiled thinly and resignedly. 'You'd better come inside,' she sighed and turned away.

Wilkie stepped inside, closed the door and followed her into the living-room, his mass seeming to diminish what was, in fact, a good-sized room.

Rachel sat down in an easy-chair, took a cigarette from the gold cigarette box on the low table and waved for Wilkie to help himself. He did so and lit both the cigarettes.

'You're a fool, Rachel,' he declared softly and wearily.

'I know it,' she agreed disinterestedly, 'but, aside from becoming involved with you, what else have I done?'

'You've talked to Shelley, my love, that's what!'

'Of course I've spoken to Simon,' she snorted in dismissal. 'But it's got him nowhere!'

'He came to ask you for a name — or any other clue — to lead him to the governor?'

'He did.'

'And you, like a fool, gave it!'

'Somebody gave you a hole in the head!' Rachel snorted. 'You and your — your 'governor' give me a severe pain! You seem to imagine you can move down here and run things the way you did in London. Well, it won't wash! This is another world. I'm outside of your sphere and I'm staying outside. I told you once to pass the word that if your boss doesn't get off my back I'll do some chirruping — loud and clear! I haven't done so yet and I won't unless I'm pushed. I'm my own woman down here — and you see to it that neither of you forget that!'

Wilkie hit her then.

That which nature had taken the better part of thirty years to grow and mould into a hard form of beauty was destroyed in a fraction of a second. Rachel could offer no defence; no reflex action could have mitigated the violence of the blow, and the chair-back had braced her head so that she could never have ridden the punch had she known it was coming.

The chair crashed over backwards and the woman rolled completely over to lie in an untidy sprawl on the expensive carpet. Rachel could not scream, her lower jaw was smashed and her left cheek-bone jutted through torn flesh. Her nose was pulp from which blood pulsed, and her mouth was a bloody mash from which her tongue tried feebly to thrust pieces of shattered teeth which bid fair to block her throat and choke her.

She was not knocked completely unconscious, but her brain had been jarred around in her skull like a reverberating echo.

'Who did you name?' Wilkie demanded, his face a ferocious mask.

Fear screamed silently back at him from the dark eyes slowly disappearing under swelling flesh and oozing blood. Rachel tried to say something, but it was no more than an incoherent mumble, her demolition had been terrifyingly effective.

'Talk, you bitch,' he hissed, moving the lighted end of his cigarette threateningly close to her eyes.

Again Rachel tried, only to be frustrated by the sheer efficiency of Wilkie's massive fist.

He reached for the nearby telephone pad and pencil and thrust them into her hands. 'Then write!' he snarled. 'Unless, of course, you want more!'

Hesitantly Rachel scrawled: 'Angela Whitney.'

Wilkie took time to decypher the scrawl and then read the name aloud in search of confirmation. Rachel nodded an affirmative.

He tore the top sheet from the pad, screwed it up and thrust it into his pocket. 'You really are a silly bitch, Rachel,' he announced, almost by way of apology. 'You could've done without the face-lift.' He raised a hand in sardonic farewell and left the flat.

Slowly Rachel's mind began to clear and to function with some of her natural cold efficiency. With difficulty she cleared her mouth to ease her breathing and then she clawed the telephone from its table. She needed help, she needed surgery and, above all else, she badly needed revenge.

She dialled 999 and set about the task of communicating with the operator.

★ ★ ★

Despite the outward signs of calm control, Stan Wilkie had become a frightened man, a fact established by the trapped animal syndrome which had made him lash out so devastatingly at Rachel Fuhrmann's face. He genuinely regretted hitting her so hard for she had been beautiful in a chiselled way and he had often fancied her as a bedmate.

It had been this desire which had allowed him to succumb to her entreaties to help her tap into his 'governor's' business interests and feather both their nests. It had been a profitable game until Rachel had stuck a speculative finger into Beverington Industrial and that 'old fool' Compton-Archer had put Simon

Shelley on the trail.

Rachel had been the one to suggest that he should report Shelley's interest to his principal and he had done so with success, but he had also learnt on which side his own bread was buttered and had allowed his association with Rachel to run down.

Now everything was coming apart unless some very drastic action could be taken.

He went into a public telephone booth, dialled a local number, inserted money and began talking earnestly. When he had finished talking he stood silent, listening to his instructions. He acknowledged them and rang off, then he walked to his car and began a late evening drive up to London.

★   ★   ★

As Elaine Rhodes crossed the concourse at Beverington station, she met Detective Constable Roger Vincent walking away from Smith's bookstall with a copy of the *Daily Telegraph* under his arm.

'Good morning, Miss Rhodes,' he said with a grin. 'After last evening's marathon I would have expected you to have a long lie-in this morning. Are you going to London?'

'Yes,' she replied cautiously, 'I am.'

'May I ask why?' he pressed.

Ordinarily Elaine would have told him where to go for asking such an impertinent question, but the circumstances were far from normal and, as a police officer, he had fair grounds for asking. 'I discovered at breakfast,' she explained, 'that my father had gone off to London on an early train and in view of his admissions of last evening I was afraid he could be doing something rather silly. I've made arrangements for my aunt to 'accidentally' drop in on Mother and spend the day with her, so I'm free to go after him.'

'There seems to be an epidemic of people rushing off to London unexpected,' Vincent observed wryly. 'Simon Shelley also went off fairly early.'

'Father was on the 6.25,' Elaine led.

'Simon caught the 7.25,' Vincent

supplied. 'Your father has a mighty long lead on me.'

* * *

Stan Wilkie left his newspaper on the dew-covered seat in the tiny patch of garden near the site of the old Roman guard-house by Tower Hill.

There was good money in that newspaper's folds and it broke his heart to leave it for the murderous, hopped-up moron who had come to sit beside him. The notice given to him by his principal had been too short for him to contact one of the better men in the 'hit-man' category and to set up the kind of cover which would be necessary. The result was that he had been obliged to make do with this expatriate Irish-American whose drug-abuse record had culminated in his being rejected out of hand by the Irish Republican Army he had come over to 'help'.

Wilkie's chief consolation was that responsibility for what was soon to happen would, in all probability, be laid at the door of terrorists rather than nervous business people.

He crossed to his car, got inside, and after yet another sigh of resignation and regret drove off on one lap of the triangular circuit by the Minories and set course back into Eastcheap. Making his way to and across Southwark Bridge, he rolled the car to a halt in a car-thieves' paradise, switched off the engine, stepped out and walked away leaving them with a sitting duck. Wilkie abandoned his car with very real regret, it was a good vehicle and had cost him the proverbial 'bomb', but, like so many of his solid assets and acquisitions, it had to go.

Elise — the girl in his Amdale office — was as silly as a rook and she'd sit there behind her desk loyally parrying enquiries for him quite long enough for him to make good his disappearance. It would take her a month of wet Sundays to realize and accept the fact that she, too, had been ditched.

Wilkie crossed back to the north side of the river and took a cab to Tothill Street, then the Underground to Baker Street. No one was following, no one appeared to care about him. He walked a quarter of a mile to the London office he held under an assumed name and there recovered from a very private place a stout manilla envelope containing his nest-egg — krugerrands, sovereigns, banknotes and three bank books in the name of Cater.

He had no regrets about leaving that office behind him; it had been no more than an address of convenience. He took the tube to Praed Street, walked up into Paddington Station and bought a single ticket to Cardiff.

On his way to the train, his mind on his purpose, he was startled to hear a once-familiar voice say: 'Good morning, Stan.'

Wilkie turned to see Ted Carteret, a railway bobby, standing there beaming at him beatifically.

'Central Office would like a word with you, me lad,' Carteret informed him.

Quickly Wilkie glanced about him trying to decide on the best direction to run. Three other, more agile, policemen were closing in. He sighed heavily and nodded. 'Okay,' he agreed.

★　★　★

Henry Rhodes placed his finger on the bellpush beside Mira Feaney's door and held it there until she opened the door.

She had been in a deep sleep until the bell dragged her to consciousness and awareness of a mounting headache and, in consequence, she was in a seething rage. She hadn't crawled into bed to sleep until the small hours after seeing her client safely onto the 3.30 a.m. train out of Euston, a connection he could never have made unaided. Mira's irritability was much in evidence even when she saw that her caller was the mild-mannered and considerate Henry Rhodes.

'You'd better come inside,' she sighed disagreeably, 'but don't get any wild notions, I'm shattered!'

He followed her into the flat, closing the door behind him. 'We're both out of luck, Mira,' he said ominously.

His tone, rather than the words, made her turn sharply and study his face intently. 'What d'ye mean?' The Waterford accents overrode the acquired English sounds.

'You've been a good girl, Mira,' said Henry. 'You've been fair and honest with me despite the bunch we're mixed up with in our various ways. So I've come to warn you that the time has come to pack up and get out; the storm is about to burst and I don't want you caught in it.'

She had more good sense than to doubt him or try to bluff him with protestations of ignorance. She showed a natural alarm, but there were no accompanying signs of panic. Quickly she placed her hands on his shoulders and kissed him affectionately. 'Thanks, Henry,' she said. 'You're a dear.'

'You'll go?' he asked urgently.

'Directly,' she assured him. 'I shan't pack much — just two light cases — and I'll be on my way.'

'Not Waterford,' Henry cautioned. 'You'd be too easy to find there.'

'No,' Mira confirmed. 'Fresh fields and pastures new.'

'Money,' Henry asked. 'You'll have enough?'

'Sure. Don't worry about me; I keep a nest-egg tucked away in a little out-of-town bank.'

He drew a wad of assorted bank notes from his pocket. It was a substantial sum and all he could readily lay hands on. 'Travelling expenses,' he said, thrusting the bundle into her hands.

Mira made no false protests; she knew Henry was doing what he considered right and proper. She took the money, guessing at its probable value. 'Like I said, Henry — you're a dear. Now, go quickly — and look after yourself.' She drew his face to hers and kissed him long in farewell. 'I'll miss you, Henry,' she told him sincerely. Then, suddenly business-like: 'Be off with you now.'

She latched the door behind him and, shaking the last veils of sleep from her brain, set to work packing her bags.

As soon as the two small pieces of hand luggage held what she needed, Mira hurriedly stepped into a brown trouser suit, threw a sheepskin coat about her shoulders and went across the corridor to the door of Angela Whitney's flat.

She pressed the bell-push, and when Angela opened the door she asked with a soft but urgent voice: 'Are you alone?'

Angela frowned. 'Yes,' she agreed, puzzled. 'Come in. I was just about to make some coffee.' She stood back to admit the Irish girl.

'Forget the coffee,' Mira urged as they went on into the livingroom. Deadly serious now, she faced Angela squarely, seeking to impress her with the importance of what she was about to say. 'A feller,' she began, 'never mind who, but a feller who knows exactly what he's about has warned me to get out of this set-up while the going's good. The edifice is about to crumble!'

'So you're taking his advice? Getting out?' Angela regretted. 'I'll miss you, Mira.'

'You might, so,' Mira agreed, 'but you'd be better advised to do the same!'

'Me? But whatever for?'

'I can't tell you that — well, not all of it. Have you ever felt the urge to pull a tin can from the bottom of the pile in a supermarket display?'

'Haven't we all?' Angela affirmed, wondering where all this was leading.

'True enough,' Mira conceded. 'Well, the people behind this organization we're in have a whole pyramid of businesses all interlinked like a pile of cans and my feller looks to me to be primed to pull out one or more of the 'cans'. If he does, you can bet your last halfpenny the reverberations will rattle through here like an earthquake!'

Still Angela failed to grasp what Mira was trying to tell her. 'I'm sorry if you mean that your 'can' will come down, Mira,' she said quietly, 'but mine's not in the pile.'

'Weren't you ever the young innocent,' Mira remarked exasperatedly. 'Will you look, child. I've been in this business long enough to know the true set-up. I won't try to explain it all to you, though, your innocence is your best shield — though I don't doubt that you probably know a good deal more than you realize. There are two names — Rousker and Fuhrmann — do they mean anything to you?'

'Well,' Angela admitted slowly, 'yes.'

'They're common to your set-up and mine. If you know them you're in danger.' She injected more urgency into her voice. 'Get out!' she implored. 'Now! In the name of God!'

Angela's lips pursed as she gave a fleeting moment to consideration and decision. A large number of odd and apparently unconnected facts suddenly gelled in her mind. It wasn't a precise and detailed picture they projected, but she intuitively accepted what they suggested. Even so, the only danger she could recognize was to her little operation.

'I've already decided to get out of this profession,' she said, 'and revert to amateur status.'

'You must be naïve or crazy, dear girl,' Mira averred. 'Girls like us don't make it back to true amateur status unless we meet the right feller *and* he doesn't know what we are. You wouldn't have such a feller, by any chance?'

'There's a man,' Angela admitted, 'and I realize I've loved him since first we met.'

'And he doesn't know?'

'He knows.'

'Then you've no chance, Angie,' Mira said, her voice soft with regret. 'Fellers simply don't marry girls like us.'

'A professional footballer may apply for a licence to play the amateur game,' Angela suggested.

'Ours is called a marriage certificate, and our controlling body is called 'Public Opinion' — you'll find it doesn't ratify a change of status so very easily.'

'Nevertheless,' returned Angela determinedly, 'I shall give it a try.'

'But you *will* leave here today?' Mira persisted. 'There's no time left for playing a reluctant fish.'

'I believe he's coming up today.'

'Then go and pack the bare essentials and leave as soon as he gets here. Whatever may come of your marriage, dreams can only happen if you get away from here.'

Angela nodded and threw a glance around her comfortable flat. She was astonished at how easily she was able to shrug off any attachment to it now that her mind was made up about Simon and events were carrying along in the direction she most wished to go. She went through to the bedroom and reached down two airweight suitcases.

The doorbell rang.

'That will be Simon,' Angela called.

'I'll go,' said Mira. 'You carry on with packing.'

She went to the door, opened it and saw a man in a brown warehouse coat. He proferred a parcel.

'Miss Whitney?' he asked.

'She's busy just now,' Mira returned, 'but I'll take it.'

The man released the parcel into her hands and turned away towards the lift.

Mira closed the door and walked into the living-room. 'Were you expecting a parcel?' she called.

Angela appeared in the bedroom doorway; she was holding a plaid skirt before her as she prepared to fold it. 'No,' she replied. 'Does it say who it's from?'

The parcel grew in the tiniest fraction

of a second, disintegrating at 3,000 feet per second, the hot gases generated by the detonation of unstable chemical atoms thrusting out, ripping and smashing all in its path. Angela never even heard the bang for she was virtually within the explosion of five pounds of Nobel's 808 blasting gelatine, and it seemed like instant hell on earth.

# 14

When Simon Shelley left the train at Victoria it was still moving, his feet hit the platform and at once he was running for the barrier and the ticket collector who stood in grimfaced judgement on his stupidity.

Simon virtually threw his half-ticket at the man and, dodging and jinking like a rugby three-quarter, he raced towards the cab-rank. He was lucky again, able to get a cab at the third attempt. A twenty-pound note hit the palm of the cabby as Simon gave him the destination and added: 'Another tenner if you set up a new record. This is *really* urgent!'

Traffic problems not withstanding, the cabby dropped him off at the foot of the steps leading to the foyer of the block where Angela lived. Simon tossed the promised ten-pound note to the driver and took the steps two at a time. Two women were emerging from the doorway, he sidestepped them and caught the doors before they could close and lock.

A lift stood waiting, doors gaping just as when the women had stepped out. Simon stepped in, thumbed the button for Angela's floor, and felt an odd judder just before the lift started upwards. When it halted again, the doors rumbled open to reveal a scene of turmoil and horror. The door of Angela's flat was propped at a crazy angle against the opposite side of the corridor and the acrid stench of explosives was in the air.

Heads were appearing in doorways, a woman screamed and another added a freak harmony to the first. A couple of men emerged from doors farther along the corridor, advanced cautiously and halted, open-mouthed with horror as they gazed at the scene from close range. The crackling sound of flames reached out to Simon, and he ran.

There was a body on the floor, not a bundle of old clothes. It was headless and armless, and one leg was so hideously twisted as to look anything but the limb of a human being.

'Angela!' he heard himself cry.

And then he saw the severed head, still unexpectedly identifiable as a dark-haired woman.

He halted and turned towards the flat doorway with its splintered frame and the inner door-frame torn from the walls and angled eccentrically across the entrance hall.

Simon turned to the two men: 'Police, Fire Brigade, Ambulance!' He ordered sharply. 'On the double!'

'Who the hell're you talking to?' one demanded belligerently.

The other nodded, turned and ran for a telephone.

A dog whimpered.

A dog?

Simon plunged through the devastated doorways and into the living-room of Angela's flat. The fire was on the point of escalation, a matter of seconds only from the moment when lethal fumes would billow from upholstery and squeeze out any life in the room. He held his breath and quickly cast about for Angela but saw no sign of her. Taking a little risk with his

307

limited air supply, he called her name twice but received no reply except a repeat of the whimpering sound. It seemed to come from the bedroom and he leapt debris to reach the shattered doorway with its crazily angled door hanging into the bedroom. Angela lay crumpled against the side of the built-in wardrobe. She seemed, at first glance, whole but grotesquely misshapen and blood seemed to ooze from numberless rents in her clothing — such as remained.

There was no time for the niceties of first aid or even reassurance, Simon scooped her up into his arms and marched boldly across the now blazing living-room with her. Her whimpering protests became little cries of unbearable agony, but he steeled his senses against them and against the heat and smoke reaching out hungrily to envelop and devour them both.

The belligerent man met him at the inner door, helping him through the entrance hall and into the corridor.

Simon carried Angela out into bedlam as people scurried this way and that like headless chickens. A few women and one man were in a state of complete panic, but the majority were trying to make an orderly business of evacuating that floor while two men and a woman advanced on the blazing flat with fire extinguishers and a first-aid hose-reel.

'Cut the electricity,' Simon gasped, and the belligerent man ran for the fuse-box on the landing of the service stairs.

'Is she alive?' an anxious voice asked.

'Just about,' Simon managed.

'We shouldn't move her.'

'I won't, after I get her downstairs,' Simon returned, heading for the lift.

Once more the belligerent man did the right thing, he cleared the lift of men, sending them off down the stairs. He ushered Simon and his burden into the lift with a number of women and sent it down.

The foyer was filling up when they reached it, and two policemen were trying, simultaneously, to calm everyone, clear a passage for expected firemen and ask questions. One of the constables spotted Simon and the blood-stained girl in his arms. At once he cleared a way to a long upholstered seat and helped ease Angela onto it.

One of the policemen radioed information on the situation before hurrying upstairs to see what he could do, and the other began doing what he could for Angela's injuries, only to draw back suddenly. 'Glass!' he exclaimed, and began again with infinitely more caution, 'What happened?' he demanded.

'An explosion followed by a fire,' Simon replied.

'Gas?'

'I think not. At a guess it was a bomb somewhere about the centre of this girl's living-room.'

'Was there a table near the centre?'

'More or less,' Simon agreed.

'With a glass vase, or something?'

'A vase.'

The policeman held up a thick chip of glass. 'She's riddled with this stuff,' he said.

Angela's lips moved, and her once-sweet voice came as a hoarse croak. 'Simon?'

'Yes,' he agreed, kneeling down and bending his head over her, the better to hear her words in the hubbub all around.

'What're you doing here?'

'I came to bring your amateur status,' he said, smiling reassuringly.

'Amateur?'

'I want you to marry me.'

She tried to shake her head. 'No,' she managed. 'Not really. It's no good, I've come to realize that.'

'It could be good,' he urged.

'No. No good,' she insisted vehemently.

'You're upsetting her, sir,' the policeman warned brusquely. 'She needs to be kept calm and still.'

'One more question,' Simon pleaded. 'It may prove important.'

'One!'

'Angela,' Simon pressed, 'who was here? We *must* know if all this is to be stopped.'

'Abe. Abe was here — ' she sucked in her breath as pain stabbed through her — 'until eight-thirty this m — ' Her eyes rolled and she fainted away.

The policeman checked her pulse.

'She's alive,' he pronounced. 'Just! Now, sir, I must insist that you stand away and let me do what I can for her.'

Firemen came and made their way up to the blazing flat; more police; an ambulance.

The ambulance crew took over with Angela, but Simon sensed they already knew they were engaged in a losing battle. He went with them to the ambulance and rode with Angela to a hospital where a weary doctor finally had to admit she was dead.

A fire of rage began as a tiny spark in Simon's belly and grew to a raging inferno before he could do anything to contain it. He wanted blood, he needed to take the perpetrator of this hideous deed and rip him limb from limb. He stared about the accident and emergency unit with blazing eyes, searching eagerly for someone or something to maim or kill, but there was nothing.

Simon let go an animal cry of frustrated rage and plunged out into a persistent downpour.

Detective Chief Inspector Jack Key-Betts looked up at Paterson. 'Go and see what we've got on Abraham Rousker, Henry Rhodes, Angela Whitney, Mira Feaney, Rachel Fuhrmann and Stanley Wilkie.'

The detective sergeant nodded and departed.

'Now,' said Key-Betts, readdressing Detective Constable Vincent. 'You believe this business pyramid may be behind a couple of beatings handed out in Beverington, right?'

Vincent nodded. 'Yes, sir, but though I have to be concerned about those beatings, I'm far more concerned about what lies behind them.'

'And rightly so,' Key-Betts approved. 'Since we received your telephone call last night we've been keeping an eye open for Wilkie and we have him in an interview-room now. He was spotted at Paddington Station and had papers and bank books which clearly gave him a choice of two alternative identities — Cater or Cowper. He intended travelling on a single ticket

313

to Cardiff and he had a large sum of ready money distributed about him.'

'He must have sensed things were about to go wrong,' Vincent mused, 'and decided to make a run for it.'

'So it would seem,' Key-Betts agreed cautiously. 'But I'd be interested to know exactly what was going wrong. He doesn't strike me as a man who would panic easily. I wonder, has he incurred someone's displeasure? And, if so, whose?'

'If someone is after him, I'd guess at Rousker or Rhodes,' Vincent said. 'Rachel Fuhrmann would be in no position to do anything.'

'Yet you declared last night that she claimed Wilkie had been the one who destroyed her face.'

'I have this feeling that he lashed out as much in fear as for any other reason,' Vincent replied. 'Rachel Fuhrmann was almost inarticulate and it was a struggle to understand her but I did get Rousker's name. This whole muddle oozes out of a mixed bag of relatively small businesses and holding companies, and two local names, in Beverington, fitted into the picture: Rhodes on the one hand — a hard-headed but straight businessman; and Abe Rousker — a genial lapsed Jew, also acknowledged as straight dealing.

'Now, a business investigator named Shelley got his nose into the edges of the set-up and got as far as Rachel Fuhrmann who, it appears, must hold some key shares — and was swiftly diverted by a crafty sabotage of his marriage. He allowed his investigations to lapse while he sorted out his private affairs and then, the original assignment long dead, had another go on his own account.'

'Why did he do that?' Key-Betts demanded suspiciously. 'Professionals rarely do something for nothing.'

Vincent shrugged. 'I suppose he wanted to know who had set him up, and why. I know I would.'

'So we have a revenge motive.'

'We have,' Vincent admitted, 'but it's made Shelley a catalyst, no more than that.'

'Maybe,' the chief inspector conceded, keeping an open mind.

'But then Shelley was beaten up by an

out-of-town duo,' Vincent said. 'We got hold of them, but either they're not talking or they don't know enough to matter.'

'The latter,' Key-Betts decided for him. 'It's par for the course.' He drew breath and went on: 'You've checked with Central Records?'

'Yes, sir, but when I left the Station this morning we were still awaiting a reply.'

Key-Betts nodded. 'I'll get someone to chase them up,' he promised. 'That pair must have some 'known associates'. But, go on with what you were saying.'

Vincent continued: 'Two names could be tied directly to the beating — other than the hired muscle, that is. The names are Rhodes and Wilkie. Rhodes was merely a business mind, of course, and it seems he employed Wilkie to find evidence to discredit Shelley in the eyes of his daughter Elaine.'

'You consider this was not the whole truth.'

Vincent nodded. 'Certainly Rhodes is hyper-protective towards his daughter, but two other factors emerged. Shelley's

316

ex-wife is working for Rhodes in a business where she is nominally manageress and he is the customer. In fact Rhodes and Rousker own the business and, from a case of embezzlement within that business, it appears Rhodes' interest in Mrs Shelley doesn't stem solely from the business connection, he has an 'emotional attachment' as they say.'

'So that gives Rhodes three reasons for wishing Shelley to hell out of it,' Key-Betts remarked.

'Abe Rousker may also have had a similar reason,' Vincent added. 'He had some connection with Rachel Fuhrmann.'

'Right, Vincent,' Key-Betts summarized, 'as I see it, you need us to supply you with a 'family tree' of these interrelated businesses in the hope it will throw up a picture in which we can find real motive, right?'

'Yes, sir.'

'And what do you expect to uncover? Some big business fiddle? Tax evasion?' Key-Betts intended to be humorous but it came over as sarcasm, and Vincent recoiled a little.

'I don't know, sir — not exactly — but I have a strong suspicion that someone, somewhere, is extremely sensitive to probing into this set-up.'

There was a rap on the door and Detective Sergeant Paterson walked in. Under his arm was a bundle of files, and these he laid on the desk before his chief.

'I suggest you read the file on Rachel Fuhrmann, sir,' he urged.

Key-Betts, a man who trusted and listened to his subordinates largely because he contrived to hand-pick them, complied.

After some moments he observed at large: 'So, our Rachel was 'done' for being on the 'game' a few years ago. Meaningless in itself, but then she seems to have settled into a 'call-girl' arrangement for a regular clientèle of provincial businessmen. She was set up in a West End flat by a syndicate of these men. Then we have rumours only of the strong-arm boys moving in to try to exploit the arrangement, only to be moved out again at the expressed wish, invitation or order of our old friend Stan Wilkie. Pat, get a warrant to search Wilkie's office — I want to know who employed him, and there's no way he's going to volunteer that information.'

'His office is now in Amdale,' Vincent cut in helpfully. 'He moved south.'

'But he still keeps a small place in the City,' Paterson countered.

'Well, we'll turn over the City office and get the names of his clients for at least five years back.'

Paterson pulled a face to show he believed it to be a pointless chore, but he knew enough to allow that Key-Betts always had a sound reason for everything he did. 'Yes, sir,' he acknowledged, and left the room.

'Rachel Fuhrmann is shown here as having a long acquaintance with your two men, Rousker and Rhodes,' Key-Betts observed to Vincent.

'Yes, sir. My information seems to confirm that.'

'Our records on her die out about eighteen months ago,' Key-Betts mused. 'Now, are we to assume that she has since tried to tread the straight and narrow?'

'Or taken up blackmail, sir?'

The chief inspector's eyes hardened and he levelled them on Vincent. 'I wonder what makes you suggest that.'

★ ★ ★

Detective Sergeant Chirter screwed up his nose as though he was passing through Billingsgate on a particularly hot day. 'A pretty thin old yarn, that,' he derided.

Simon Shelley shrugged off the expressed doubts. 'You'll find it checks out,' he declared. 'Take your time, put some men onto investigating it. Or accept the truth for what it is and get on to pulling in your killer.'

'We may already have him,' Chirter replied. 'You could have planted the bomb, gone away, then doubled back choc full of innocence.'

'Where did I learn to make such a bomb?' Simon challenged confidently. 'Where did I get the explosive?'

'You could be IRA.'

'I'm not,' Simon asserted, 'and you know it, so why mention it?'

'Characteristics of the bomb. A typically small terrorist device. *And* one of the women was Irish.'

'They weren't after Mira Feaney,' Simon averred. 'Irish she may have been but they were after Angela Whitney.'

'You know a helluva lot for an innocent man,' Chirter snorted.

'Angela Whitney was a valuable link in my investigations. It's my belief she had some knowledge which could have cracked things wide open and she had to be silenced.'

'Explain,' Chirter demanded.

'Are you really interested?' Simon doubted.

'Just give me the explanation.'

'I was investigating a small group of businesses,' Simon began. 'We can fill in detail later, but what it boils down to is this: 'An informant, Rachel Fuhrmann, gave me the hint that Angela Whitney could be my next lead, and Rachel was beaten up for talking to me. The man who beat her up is named Wilkie.'

'Stan Wilkie?' Chirter cut in. 'He can be a real hard man, and thumping a woman in line with what he might see as his duty is about par for the course.'

He felt it unnecessary to mention that there was already a call out for Wilkie, wanted for questioning by the Yard.

Simon continued: 'It's my belief that after dealing with Rachel Fuhrmann Wilkie called his principal and explained what had happened. The result was that he was ordered to 'see off' Angela Whitney.'

'Why not Mira Feaney?' Chirter posed. 'She copped it worse than the other girl!'

'She was just plain unlucky,' Simon asserted. 'You *know* she was unlucky. She just happened to be in Angela's flat.'

'Coincidence,' Chirter suggested, testing the ground.

Simon shrugged. 'It happens.'

'Sit tight,' Chirter directed and got to his feet. He gathered up his papers and walked from the room.

★   ★   ★

Detective Inspector Deeting was tired — exhausted, in fact. He'd had a bad and busy night and it was his considered opinion that two hours was insufficient time in bed for a tired and ageing policeman — he was all of thirty-five, and it showed.

'The girl, Angela Whitney,' he recapped wearily to Chirter, 'reportedly said that 'Abe was here' and that he left at eight-thirty this morning. Abe who?'

'Rousker,' Chirter supplied. 'Shelley says it would be Abe Rousker, a Beverington businessman.'

'There's also this Rachel Fuhrmann and Stan Wilkie in the picture,' Deeting mused. 'You're checking with Records?'

'Yes, sir. And there's a call out for Wilkie — the Yard want a word with him.'

'Oh?' Deeting snapped awake. 'Who put out the call?'

'Detective Chief Inspector Key-Betts, sir?'

'When?'

'Last night, sir.'

'Last night?' Deeting protested. 'Does someone have something against me?'

'You had enough on your plate, sir,' Chirter defended.

Deeting screwed up his nose at the memory. 'Yes,' he agreed meditatively. 'Get Key-Betts on the blower,' he directed Chirter, 'I have a feeling.'

And when Edward James Deeting had a feeling —

Chirter picked up the telephone. After a while he got through to Key-Betts and passed the telephone to Deeting.

'Jack? Ted Deeting here. I believe you're after Stan Wilkie.'

'Ah, good morning, Ted. Wilkie we already have — a railway bobby spotted him at Paddington all set to take off for distant parts, complete with two false identities.'

'May I ask why you're interested in him?' Deeting pressed.

'Probable accessory to fraud, but we're holding him pro tem on an assault charge.'

'Rachel Fuhrmann?' Deeting hazarded.

'Hey! Are you looking over my shoulder? I have her file on my desk!'

Deeting took a decision. 'I've got myself a murder,' he said, 'and it seems to me our paths are converging. Suppose I gather up my witnesses and move in with you while we get to the bottom of this?'

'Good idea,' Key-Betts agreed. 'I'll put the kettle on.'

# 15

Ted Deeting was feeling better, even his tiredness seemed to have evaporated. He had a motive of sorts for the murder of Angela Whitney and Mira Feaney, and Key-Betts' team were still turning up the 'building bricks' from which was made the broad-based business pyramid at whose apex stood the figure behind the murders.

Interview-rooms and offices were littered with people able to help with enquiries and the whole scene was one of confusion where none existed.

Files on terrorists had thrown up the name of Jake Tyler, one-time bomb-maker in an IRA group but long since dropped by them as being too unreliable, and he had also gone onto the drugs scene. The characteristics of the murder bomb fitted his style exactly. Knowing who to look for was one thing — finding him, quite another.

Key-Betts looked into the room he had borrowed for Deeting and his team. 'Ted,' he said, 'the general business picture is clarifying further. It's almost certain that Abe Rousker is your man.'

'Rousker? Earlier you thought he was just a small man in this — rather like that Rhodes character!'

'And that's how it looked,' Key-Betts returned. 'Even Jack Scott thought so when we spoke to him but, as the pyramid comes to a peak we're running into the name A. R. Rousker with increasing frequency.'

'That's great,' said Deeting. 'Now I have one for you. Rhodes was 'getting it' from Mira Feaney and he made a special journey up to town on an early train this morning.'

Key-Betts sighed. 'Just when I thought we'd narrowed the field!'

Deeting shrugged resignedly. 'I've got a call out for both Rhodes and Rousker,' he said. 'We'll see what they have to say for themselves.'

'And in the meantime,' Key-Betts suggested, 'what d'you say we have another go at Stan Wilkie?'

Deeting nodded. It was worth a try.

★ ★ ★

'We know about you and Jake Tyler,' Deeting announced bluntly when Wilkie again sat before him. 'He'll be picked up soon. Now, d'you feel like unburdening yourself?'

'About what?' Wilkie asked interestedly.

'About you contracting Tyler to kill Angela Whitney.'

'Did I do that?'

'You did.'

Wilkie smiled indulgently. 'I'm glad the onus of proof is on you,' Wilkie beamed, 'especially as I don't know anyone by the name of Jake Tyler.'

'Perhaps not by name,' Deeting conceded, 'but you were certainly rushing around town during the night, searching for someone to deal with the girl, but none of the established hit-men wanted to know, did they?'

'Don't ask me, old son,' returned Wilkie. 'This is *your* story. I don't know how it goes.'

Deeting ignored the sally and went on: 'You were becoming desperate to get the job done today, and when somebody put you onto Tyler as a last resort you leapt in with both feet and no brains.'

'I don't know anyone by that name,' Wilkie sighed wearily. 'I did tell you!'

'So you did,' Deeting agreed equably, 'and I believe you. But you know exactly what he was.'

'One case of GBH doesn't make me an habitual,' Wilkie cautioned.

'But you procured plenty of thumpings,' Deeting asserted.

'So you say,' said Wilkie. 'Why didn't you arrest me?'

'Because we couldn't prove *those*,' Deeting replied pointedly.

'Even if you could prove them, they don't make me a killer.'

'I don't believe you set out to have the girl killed,' Deeting conceded. 'You probably intended her to be knee-capped, in the first place, but as you slipped down the list of possibles, you ran into greater danger of bagging an unreliable psycho.

In the end you had only Jake Tyler left
— killer, bomb expert, psychopath and
drug addict — and you gave instructions
that he was to 'deal' with Angela Whitney.
The trouble was that from then on you
lost control of the affair and by that time
you knew Angela Whitney was as good as
dead so you set out to 'disappear' before
that could happen. Unfortunately for you,
the Beverington police already wanted
you for the attack on Rachel Fuhrmann.'

Wilkie sneered openly. 'Conjecture,' he
jeered. 'There's nothing to prove!'

'Tyler will tell us.'

'How the hell can he?' Wilkie challenged confidently. 'We've never met, I
never set up any deal. Your only chance
— assuming you find the man — is to
bribe or blackmail him to put the finger
on me.'

'But you did beat up Rachel Fuhrmann,' Deeting insisted.

'Of course I belted Rachel in the
mouth,' Wilkie agreed, much as one
humours a child, 'she had it coming in
one way or another, but that doesn't
mean I'm involved in this other affair.'

'Why did she have it coming?'

'Blackmail. She was putting the bite on me.'

Deeting and Key-Betts exchanged glances. Both knew their man and both knew he was lying.

'What does she have on you?' Key-Betts pressed.

'Why the hell should I tell you?'

'As an earnest of the rest of your story,' Deeting suggested.

Wilkie shrugged. 'She said she'd spread the word that I was sleeping with Elise — my receptionist.'

'Were you?'

'Of course I was!'

'And in this day and age when sleeping around is almost a social requirement, you felt you had to knock her teeth down her throat?'

Wilkie gave another shrug. 'She needed to be shown just what the blackmailer's reward felt like — she had the naive notion that it felt like paper money.'

Key-Betts pulled an expression of distaste and addressed the constable standing at the door. 'Wheel this thing back to the detention-room,' he said.

As the door closed on prisoner and escort, he said to Deeting: 'The keys are Shelley and Rousker. That woman told Shelley something — not much, perhaps, but enough. Wilkie went to her knowing that she'd talked. Only Shelley could have told anyone else and we need to know who.'

'I'll fetch Shelley in again,' Deeting decided.

★   ★   ★

Simon was stiff and tired, and bored with just sitting about helpless to do a thing to get things moving. His interest in revenge had lost its initial impetus and now he just longed to go home and call Elaine. For a moment he wondered if he was being disloyal to Angela's memory, but then he knew he wasn't. She had returned to him the ability to love — something taken from him by Marion — and he had found Elaine, a maturing woman naïve in the ways of love but eager to learn, enjoy and give freely of her own loving nature.

Angela had made him the priceless gift of love and he must not now squander it.

He sat, stolidly patient, in the office shared by two detective sergeants. The sergeants had been in and out of the room without paying him much attention, and other people had added to the activity. They had talked, all of them, ignoring the presence of the dejected man in the corner.

A new crop arrived.

'Tyler's turned up,' one man supplied. 'The search team found him jammed in an airshaft in the flats. He'd fallen down from the top and his neck was broken.'

Simon's mind registered the fact that he was off the hook though the name of Tyler meant nothing to him in itself.

Another policeman entered the room and stood before him. 'Would you come with me, please, Mr Shelley?' The politeness was formal, but Simon thought he noted a softening of the tone.

Simon followed along corridors to the office where Key-Betts and Deeting waited. Did he detect here, too, a subtle change?

'Sit down, Mr Shelley,' said Key-Betts, smiling reassuringly. 'We'd like to ask you some more questions.'

Simon nodded, but said nothing.

'You pressed Rachel Fuhrmann for a clue,' Deeting opened, 'or maybe some other help. We know why; we now wish to know how.'

'I told her that if she didn't give me a worthwhile lead to whoever was behind my beating — and all the other troubles — I'd tell Detective Constable Vincent of the connection between her and Wilkie. I also told her Vincent was not the man to let up once he got his teeth into something.'

'What was their connection?' Deeting pressed. He believed he knew more about that connection than Shelley but, of course, he was not fool enough to make it apparent.

'Simple enough,' Simon replied, 'opposite sides of the fence. I'd been told by Wilkie's receptionist at his Amdale office that Rachel was putting the black on his principal.'

'Why would she do that?'

Simon looked up dully at Deeting. 'Rachel?'

'The receptionist.'

'Wilkie sent her after me after he'd refused to tell me anything directly.'

'Why would he do that?' demanded Key-Betts.

'A fake olive branch — 'I'm on your side but I mustn't be obvious'. You can guess at the picture.'

Deeting nodded. 'And *was* she putting the black on his client?'

Simon shrugged. 'I'm not certain. If she was, I believe Rachel would be doing it in self-defence, not as a mercenary deal.'

'What gives you that idea?'

'I can only guess,' Simon warned. 'Rachel had worked in London as a call-girl. She was paid, or received as gifts, a number of company shares. She's no fool and she figured a way to improve her position by arranging to be paid out in shares wherever she could. Somewhere along the line she trod on someone's toes and wound up working for that person in this new form of doing business. She graduated to manageress of a call-girl organization principally aimed at bleeding shares and business information out of carefully selected clients who believed themselves to be members of small syndicates keeping girls exclusively on tap.

'Rachel continued to pick up shares on her own account and not long ago achieved at least one major holding. Her boss demanded that Rachel reduce her holding — or else. But Rachel, scared though she was, knew the real strength of her position. In effect, she said, 'Leave me be or I'll tell the whole story.' She may even have put her story in writing and left it with a solicitor — I don't really know — but whichever way it went, she held out.'

'Until you got Angela Whitney's name out of her.'

'Yes. After that there could be no more delays,' Simon agreed.

'You told someone what Rachel Fuhrmann had told you,' Key-Betts said. 'Who?'

'Abe Rousker. At least, I told his wife to

warn him off. He'd already left.'

'Why tell him?'

'I knew that he was going to see Angela and I wanted to warn him to get out of the mess while he could. I thought he was just a small can in the pile, and anyway, I owed him something.'

'We know Rousker's not just a little man in this — that picture was his protection — we've built up a more complete picture and he fills top spot,' declared Key-Betts.

'Abe?' Simon doubted loyally. 'You'll have a hard time convincing me of that!'

Key-Betts waved a hand, inviting Simon to look at the green baize-covered board on the wall where small cards built up like a pyramid with only a few building blocks missing.

Simon rose and turned wearily to face the board. He saw Abe Rousker's name in the lower tiers. He ran his gaze up through the holding companies to the narrowing picture towards the summit and again the name of Rousker became prominent.

Simon's mind ranged back over the

years he'd known Abe and Becky Rousker, and in particular he recalled their freely given friendship and affection. He remembered, too, the sense of shock when Becky had told him of her acceptance of Abe's philandering and of her actual provision of women for him and his business acquaintances. He looked again at the base and summit, taking more note of detail.

'Rousker, you said?' he asked innocently.

'Plain enough. Here, here, here . . . ' Key-Betts' finger moved about the foundations and then moved to the top. 'Here, here and here — where it matters most!'

Simon shook his head. 'You've got it wrong,' he asserted. 'Down here it's 'A. Rousker' . . . up here it's 'A. R. Rousker' . . . '

'Just a matter of the second initial,' Deeting suggested.

'I've known the Rouskers a long time,' Simon countered. 'We've been real friends and friends talk about families and things like that.'

'So?' Key-Betts was totally interested. He noted the sadness dulling Shelley's tone and the slump of his shoulders. Shelley, he knew, was about to do his duty but it was going to mean stabbing a life-time friend in the back — and that was really hurting.

'Abraham Rousker is his name,' Simon sighed. '*All* of it!'

Key-Betts shrugged. 'So he added an initial . . . '

'Abe Rousker's wife was named after her mother, Alicia,' Simon muttered, his mind numbing. 'Having the same name caused difficulties at home and the family fell to using her second name — Rebecca — shortened to Becky.'

Key-Betts sighed resignedly. 'Alicia Rebecca Rousker,' he mused. 'A. R. Rousker . . . '

'She ran the call-girl business and through the girls acquired the shares which gave her total control of Abe's business affairs by one route or another. If I'd got to Angela and she'd told me all she knew, I'd've been onto this game sooner,' Simon averred sadly, 'but I told

Becky and she gave Wilkie his orders to move Angela off the scene. He couldn't refuse but even he didn't like what was happening and after setting up the deal, he bolted.'

Key-Betts stood up and addressed Deeting. 'Let's go get Becky Rousker,' he decided.

* * *

Elaine Rhodes snuggled comfortably against Simon Shelley as the train leapt through the night towards Beverington. It had been a day of tragedy, but at last the wearying turmoil had calmed and she and Simon had been left to their own devices.

'What time does the train get in?' she asked.

'About one a.m., I believe,' he said. 'If you're tired, I'm sorry, but we could have stayed up in London.'

She shook her head. 'No. That wouldn't do,' she returned. 'I need to be with you tonight and it has to be in our own bed — *your* bed — '

Simon's finger on her lips halted her.

340

'*Our* bed,' he insisted. He had the strangest feeling that Angela would understand.

## THE END

# THE GUILTY WITNESSES

## John Newton Chance

Jonathan Blake had become involved in finding out just who had stolen a precious statuette. A gang of amateurs had so clever a plot that they had attracted the attention of a group of international spies, who habitually used amateurs as guide dogs to secret places of treasure and other things. Then, of course, the amateurs were disposed of. Jonathan Blake found himself being shot at because the guide dogs had lost their way . . .

# THIS SIDE OF HELL

## Robert Charles

Corporal David Canning buried his best friend below the burning African sand. Then he was alone, with a bullet-sprayed ambulance containing five seriously injured men and one hysterical nurse in his care. He faced heat, dust, thirst and hunger; and somewhere in the area roamed almost two hundred blood-crazed tribesmen led by a white mercenary with his own desperate reasons for catching up with the sole survivors of the massacre. But Canning vowed that he would win through to safety.

# HEAVY IRON

## Basil Copper

In this action-packed adventure, Mike Faraday, the laconic L.A. private investigator, stumbles by accident into one of his most bizarre and lethal cases when he is asked to collect a fifty thousand dollar debt by wealthy club owner, Manny Richter. Instead, Mike becomes involved in a murderous web of death, crime and corruption until the solution is revealed in the most unexpected manner.